The S.O.S. Boys in...

Mystery on Orcas Island

Written by Rosanna I. Porter

Illustrated by Tessa Asato

Library of Congress Cataloging in Publication Data

Porter, Rosanna I., Author
Asato, Tessa, Illustrator

The S.O.S. Boys in ... Mystery on Orcas Island

Summary: Rick, Greg, and Topher are the S.O.S. Boys who along with
Aaron, an Irish Setter, solve two mysteries while crab fishing near
Orcas Island, WA. The mysteries involve an alien dog and a gold heist.

[1. Science fiction mystery adventure. 2. Childhood responsibility and
learning. 3. Orcas Island. 4. Crab Fishing. 5. Markarian Galaxy]

ISBN 978-0-982- 55305-3 (paperback)
Typesetting, Composition Digital Imaging: Raisykinder Publishing

Editorial Review: Dr. Gaye L. Green

Printed in the United States of America by:

M&K Publishing
Mike McCoy
888-897-9693   mike@mandkpublishing.com
** Specializing in hard cover and paperback books, catalogs, and magazines **
www.mandkpublishing.com

Dedication.....

Though this story is set on a real island in the Puget Sound of Washington, no actual Orcas Island residents make their appearance in the story. Although some of the actual places mentioned in the story are real on Orcas Island, they may have been embellished, while others were created to add interest. I hope the residents of Orcas Island will forgive me for taking these liberties and enjoy their island being set as the stage for the S.O.S. Mystery Book Series.

I would also like to acknowledge my husband, Rick, who patiently read through the story and offered great suggestions!

Rosanna

These fun illustrations are dedicated to my awesome best friend and boyfriend, Nate. Thanks for always being there for me and inspiring me to always do my best.

Tessa

All characters appearing in this work are fictitious. Any resemblance to real persons, living or dead, is purely coincidental. The Irish Setter, Aaron; however, is real. The alien dog, Markie, you will have to decide for yourself.

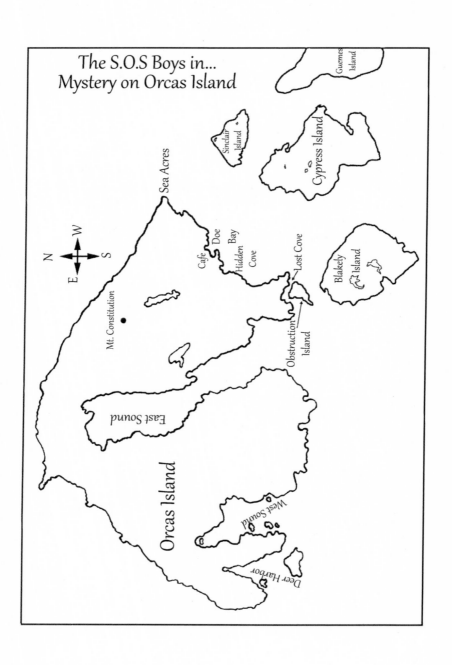

Chapter 1

"Catch!" said Rick as he threw Topher his life jacket.

"Settle down boy," ordered Greg as he put Aaron's life jacket on him. Aaron was Rick's Irish Setter. The boys always wore their life jackets when they went out in their boat and they always put one on Aaron. The waters could be choppy out on the bay.

The boys were on their way from their house and docks on the mainland near the city of Bellingham to their parents' cabins on Orcas Island. Their house on the mainland is located in Dragon Cove. It is called Dragon Cove because the outline of the cove looks like a head of a dragon. There is a small island called Eye Island which is located where the eye of the dragon would be if the outline of Dragon Cove is viewed from high above on the surrounding cliffs.

"Today, it is going to be a great day out on the water," commented Greg.

"Yeah, there are no winds and the sun is out!" replied Topher.

Rick added, "We'll make good time. I am guessing we should be there by lunch time."

The water was glistening as the boys set a course for Orcas Island. The boat glided along as they cranked up the engine to nearly full throttle. They were making excellent time on the relatively smooth water.

"Aarf, aarf, aarf!" barked Aaron, as he anxiously paced around in their 16-foot boat.

"Yeah boy, we are getting close to the island. Our dock is just around the next turn," replied Rick.

"He sure is excited about something," said Greg.

Then all of a sudden, W – O – O – S – H ... something swam quickly under their boat. The boat bounced around a lot on the water from whatever had swum under it.

"Wow! What was that?" asked Topher.

"It couldn't have been an orca," answered Greg. "It was traveling way too fast!"

"It had to have been a seal," said Rick. "Although, I have never had a seal make the boat bounce around that much. Hopefully, an orca whale is not chasing the seal."

Aaron hung his head down over the side of the boat trying to get a scent. He started barking and running around in the little boat again.

The boys kept watching the water to see if something

would surface farther out, but all they could see was a ripple of something moving very fast under the water and away from their boat. The boys turned around to make sure that an orca was not behind them chasing the seal --- or whatever it was. They certainly did not want to be in-between an orca and its prey.

"Phew, no orca!" they all said with relief.

Topher added, "I was out on the water last week when the J pod of orcas swam about 100 feet from the boat. I turned off the engine, so I wouldn't disturb them. They glided along and it was fun to watch them breach on the water. The boat barely moved even when they were splashing and breaching."

The boys knew whale watchers and local marine biologists assign each pod of orcas an alphabetical letter. This helps them to keep track of the orcas as they move around the islands of the Puget Sound. The boys were familiar with the pods that move with regularity around the islands – especially those that travel around Orcas Island. These orca pods are known as resident pods, since they stay within the Puget Sound year-round. Each orca has unique markings on their saddle patch next to the base of their dorsal fin and these markings help whale watchers identify the different orcas and their pods. The older females lead each pod or family of orcas around the islands in search of food. Everyone usually tries to get a glimpse of the orcas, so they can identify the pod. Sometimes there is more than one pod traveling together.

As the boys sailed around the rocky outcrop to their little cove called Hidden Cove, they steered towards the dock. Aaron had finally settled down and the boys prepared to dock the boat.

After they secured the boat with a line on the dock, they began to get their gear out of the boat. Then suddenly, Aaron got spooked again, ran to the end of the dock, and started to bark.

"Aaron, are you still giving that seal a piece of your mind? I think that seal is long gone," said Topher, and the boys laughed in agreement.

"Come on Aaron," ordered Rick. "We have to get our gear into the cabin and get lunch."

Aaron snorted at the water and then turned and ran towards the boys. His tail was wagging because he knew a good lunch would be waiting for him.

As the boys entered the cabin, they saw a note from Rick's mom on the kitchen counter.

Rick,

There is pizza in the refrigerator for you and the guys. Bake the pizza for 10-15 minutes at 400 degrees. Don't let Aaron eat too many pizza bones. I have other meals for you in the refrigerator.

Text me after you read this note, so I know you made it to Orcas Island!

Oh! And there are homemade cookies in the cookie jar.

See you in a couple of days.

Love,

Mom

Rick quickly texted is mom ---

Made it, all is OK.

Greg and Topher also texted their moms they had arrived safely on the island.

Topher looked into the refrigerator and said, "Rick, your mom put a ton of food in here. I don't think we are going to starve. I'll get the pizza out. "

Greg turned on the oven and Topher put the pizza in the oven. Aaron started jumping around in hopeful anticipation for those wonderful pizza bones that would be tossed to him from the boys. A pizza bone is what the boys called the crust of the pizza. Aaron liked the pieces that had cheese or tomato sauce smeared on them. When the pizza was ready, the boys sat down to eat.

After they finished eating the pizza, Rick said, "Boy, I was really hungry."

Topher and Greg nodded in agreement. Aaron just moaned in satisfaction. Then, they walked over and grabbed cookies from the cookie jar. Out the door they went to check out the shoreline and to pick up driftwood. Tonight, they were going to build a bonfire and make s'mores.

Their parents usually came out on the weekends and since it was only Wednesday, the boys had three days on their own. At 15 years old, it was an adventure when they came out ahead of their parents. They had been going to Orcas Island since they were born. Last year, the boys started arriving a day ahead of their parents and this summer, they were going to try to stay most of the time on the island.

There was a lot to explore on the island, but first they

had to prove to their parents they were able to take care of themselves and be responsible. Sometimes that was easier said than done, but now they were motivated and that motivation was called, freedom.

"Hey guys, come here!" yelled Rick. "You have to check out these strange marks in the sand."

Topher and Greg ran over to where Rick was standing. The boys looked at a set of four marks equally placed in the sand.

"What the heck is that?" asked Topher. "It looks like a four-legged animal would have been standing there, but the tracks are not like an animal."

Greg added, "It almost looks like a table because the marks are kind of square with a strange ridge around the same side on all four legs or posts."

"Wow, look at the tracks farther out on the beach. The legs seem to spread apart, almost like something that is running," commented Rick. "Look at Aaron's tracks as he runs along on the beach. See how they are spread out."

Aaron heard his name and ran over to where the boys were standing. He started to smell the sand and dig his paw into the sand as if he was trying to get something out.

"Let's follow the tracks and see where they go," said Greg.

They followed the tracks around the corner until they came to another little cove. Aaron, with his head down, was following the tracks with his nose. When he got to the end of the tracks, he started barking at the water and pacing anxiously around. The tracks went directly into the water. The tide was out and they did not see the tracks come back out of the water anywhere else on the beach.

"That is weird," added Rick. "The tracks are recent too."

"It's probably Matt and his little brother, Thomas, trying to be funny by walking on stilts on the sand," said Topher. "They are always playing pranks on everyone on the island, but you would think there would be footprints coming back out of the water."

"Maybe, they had their boat in the water and walked over to it, got in, and sailed away," reasoned Greg.

"Hmm, that's true," said the boys in reply.

They started sharing past Matt and Thomas pranks that the boys had played on the islanders over the years.

Greg said, "We need to think of a good one to play on them!"

Rick and Topher liked that idea.

"Well for now, let's get our wood set-up by the fire pit and then, get changed to go for a swim," said Topher.

The boys ran over and picked up their driftwood they had gathered and headed back to the fire pit. They stacked their wood and got the bonfire set-up for their evening bonfire. Even Aaron had a large stick that he added to the pile.

The boys were going to stay at Rick's cabin until their parents arrived on the island on Saturday morning.

The boys walked over to the little cove where they had followed the tracks earlier and decided to snorkel and swim in the cove. The water was not deep and they could always see interesting sea life on the cove floor. A small rocky outcrop protected the cove from too much wake action caused by passing boats and since the cove was not deep they didn't need to worry about any orcas going into the cove in search of food.

As they were snorkeling, they followed the tracks again, but noticed they had suddenly stopped. Topher, popped his head up and said, "Just as I thought, Matt and Thomas must have gotten into their boat."

Since the sun was starting to set on the water, the boys decided to get dry clothes on and start their bonfire. They were going to cook hot dogs outside over the fire, toast their marshmallows, and eat s'mores. Aaron was looking forward to the hot dogs served over his kibble.

After changing, the boys headed out of the cabin with a bag of potato chips, a package of hot dogs, cans of pop, and all the ingredients to make s'mores tucked under their arms. They sat on large logs that encircled the fire pit roasting their hot dogs. They had picked up several long and slender sticks they could use as a spear to cook their hot dogs. They had several hot dogs on each of their sticks. Rick had a few extra hot dogs for Aaron on his stick. Aaron sat next to him patiently watching his hot dogs cook. Drool started to pour from his mouth.

"Hey guys, look at Aaron. If we need to put the fire out quickly, we can have Aaron stand over it and drool on it," joked Rick.

"Gross," they both replied with a laugh.

Aaron only barked as if to say, "I don't care how it is cooked; I just want mine now."

They ate their hot dogs right from the sticks, no napkins, silverware, or plates were necessary and most importantly no clean up either!

"Boy, this is the way to eat," said Topher.

They were talking and planning what they were going to do the next day as the sun set over the cliff on the opposite side of their little cove.

"Time for s'mores!" declared Greg.

Topher and Greg were putting their marshmallows on their sticks. Rick was busy counting out the chocolate bars.

"Twelve! We can each have four chocolate bars," calculated Rick. "We will have to get more chocolate bars at the store in Doe Bay tomorrow."

Aaron started to pace around and acted agitated. "Don't worry boy, I've brought your chew bone. Here it is."

Rick handed Aaron his chew bone, but he wouldn't take it. Instead, he just kept pacing and whimpering.

"You sure are getting spooked a lot lately," said Greg to Aaron.

"Boy, there must be a seal in the water teasing him," said Topher.

Topher shined his flashlight over towards the water and the cliff above it and said, "I don't see anything."

He then went back to roasting his marshmallows.

Then, within a few seconds, Rick said, "Did you see that? Two bright lights just flashed back to us from the cliff -- over there. Look!" He pointed towards the cliff across from them.

Topher and Greg looked up, but they didn't see

anything.

"If you are trying to distract us from our chocolate bars, it isn't going to work," laughed Topher. "Greg, be careful. I think Aaron and Rick are teaming up against us!"

"No really, there it goes again. Look!" yelled Rick.

The boys looked up, but didn't see anything. Instead, they looked at each other and nodded like they knew there was some kind of devious plot going on between Rick and Aaron.

Rick kept looking up at the cliff, but didn't see the lights any more. So he went back to a more serious task at hand --- s'mores.

Aaron settled down and started to chew on his bone. Then suddenly, he jumped up again with his nose in the air as if he were trying to get the scent of something. Topher saw him and said as he directed his flashlight at the cliff and water, "See, nothing at all." Then, two lights flashed back at him and this time Topher saw it.

"What the heck was that?" he said. "Two lights just flashed back at me. Did you see that?"

"No, I didn't," said Greg.

Rick quickly said, "No, I didn't see it, but now do you believe me?"

"Shine your flashlight again," ordered Greg. "Maybe it will flash back again and I can see it."

Topher shined his flashlight on the cliff. The boys sat and waited to see what would happen. With their eyes fixed on the cliff, two lights flashed back at them. It looked like two flashlights blinking back and forth. Then, the lights changed to a red color and then a green color. The boys just sat there with their mouths open. No one spoke for a few minutes.

"Answer back to whomever is flashing lights at us," said Rick.

"Answer back, what?" asked Topher.

Greg replied, "I don't know, just start turning your flashlight off and on and wave it around. Let's see what happens."

Topher did as Greg had suggested, but there were no more lights flashing from the cliff.

"Who do you think it was?" asked Topher.

Then suddenly, Rick cupped his hands around his mouth and yelled, "We see you Matt!"

"Did you really see Matt?" questioned Greg.

"No, but it probably is him fooling around with us. I wanted him to know that we knew it was him. Otherwise, he will go into town and tell everyone he scared us. I can't let him get away with that one," stated Rick with conviction.

Every once in a while they would look over at the cliff, but no more lights flashed back at them that evening. It started to get late, the fire was out and cold, and so the boys walked up to the cabin to go to sleep. It was a busy day and they were tired.

As were most of the cabins on the island, Rick's parents' cabin was an A-frame and on the top floor was the dormitory. The dormitory was where the kids always slept. It was a huge room with six twin beds. It had a large bathroom attached, a walk-in closet, and a picture window that overlooked the water and clearing. The three bedrooms on the first floor were for the adults.

The kids always liked to stay in the dormitory because they could talk all night and their parents couldn't hear them – or at least they thought they couldn't.

As they crawled into their beds, Greg said between yawns, "Tomorrow, we should go over to the cliff and check it out. Maybe, we can see if there are any tracks over there."

In a very sleepy response, Topher and Rick agreed it was a good idea. Aaron laid down on the carpet by Rick's bed, waiting for him to fall asleep so he could sneak onto Rick's bed.

Sometime in the night, Aaron got up when he heard something outside the window. He put his paws up on the window and started to scratch at it. He looked around, but the boys didn't hear him. He just stood there looking out the window at what was looking in at him and the boys. When it went away, he went back to sleep with Rick.

Chapter 2

The boys slept in and when they finally got up, they were ready to start their day. Since they slept with their clothes on, they were ready to go outside and check out the cliff soon after breakfast. As they stepped out of the cabin, they didn't have to go far before they saw their first set of tracks. Directly outside the door past the walkway were the same strange marks they had seen yesterday in the sand on the beach. They followed the tracks to the side of the house. Whatever it was the tracks just stopped and then appeared to move around in the same spot for a while.

"Why would the tracks stop here and move around like this?" asked Rick.

"I don't know," answered Greg and Topher. "What

would they or it have been doing here? There isn't anything here except the side of the house," added Topher.

Aaron was now sniffing around and then jumped up on his two hind legs. He placed his front paws on the cabin's siding. He appeared to be trying to pick up a scent farther up the wall. The boys saw what he was doing and followed his gaze upward.

"Whoa, look there are two large scratch marks on the siding near the dormitory window! The scratches are almost eight feet above the ground!" said Greg in a shocked tone.

Rick said, "You know, Aaron got up last night and was scratching at the window. I just ignored him because I thought he was just getting spooked again. He must have heard something and was trying to tell us."

"Do you think whoever it was might have been looking into our window last night?" asked Greg. "It would be difficult because it is up one whole floor!"

"Gosh, I don't think that even Matt would do something like this. Do you guys?" Topher asked.

The boys just shook their heads as if they weren't sure what to think.

"Let's get our backpacks and check out the cliff area," suggested Rick. "Then afterwards, we can head into Doe Bay. Let's have lunch at the Doe Bay Café and talk to Mr. Hamilton about the crabbing job. He said he could use us to catch crabs for his café this summer."

The boys agreed and were eager to get answers to the strange happenings that seemed to be going on.

Also, they were looking forward to working for Mr. Hamilton and earning extra money this summer.

With their backpacks on, the boys and Aaron headed off to the cliff area. They couldn't go by way of the shoreline because the tide was in. Instead, they had to walk the long way around to the cliff. It was a densely covered area with native vegetation. Whatever the lower brush didn't cover the Madrona trees filled in. There wasn't much to see and the trail was a dead-end and for these reasons local kids rarely climbed this cliff. They kept looking down at the ground hoping to see something. They were hoping to see footprints or anything that would easily explain the lights they had seen last night and the tracks this morning in front and at the side of the cabin.

Aaron put his head down and started running off ahead of the boys into the thicker part of the wooded area. The boys could hear him as he went running through the brush.

"Rabbit scent, most likely," reasoned Rick.

The boys just nodded their heads as they kept looking down for any kind of signs of something – anything. They got to the spot where they thought the lights were coming from and when they did – they saw the same strange marks in the dirt they had seen on the beach and near the cabin this morning.

Topher was the first to see the marks, "Hey guys, check this out! The same marks are here."

They both walked over and looked down.

"Whoa, that is weird. There aren't any other marks in the dirt other than these," remarked Rick. "Where did Aaron go?" Without hesitating Rick began to whistle and yell, "Come on Aaron."

Aaron didn't come. Rick began to get a little anxious, "Come on Aaron!" Still nothing. "Aaron, hamburger!"

In a matter of seconds, the boys could hear him running towards them. They were happy to hear him bounding through the woods with twigs cracking and his four paws thumping along.

"This all seems a little suspicious," commented Topher.

Rick and Greg shook their heads in agreement. Slowly and carefully they made their way back to their clearing.

"Let's take the boat over to Doe Bay, eat lunch, and then talk to Mr. Hamilton about the crabbing job," said Rick.

With their life jackets on, the boys and Aaron jumped into their boat. They set a course for Doe Bay. It was a wonderful sunny day. As they were traveling towards Doe Bay, they were discussing where they would put their crab pots and hoping that Mr. Hamilton would let them catch crabs for his café.

"Last year, I put some crab pots just over there," Greg said as he pointed to a little area off the starboard side of the boat, "and it was like a gold mine. I caught tons of crabs for my parents."

"Cool," replied Rick, "it will be great to earn extra money this summer. Maybe we could earn enough money to get a little bigger boat."

The boys had worked a lot of odd jobs for two years to be able to pool their money together and buy the little boat they shared. Also, they continued to work to earn gas money.

"Or," added Topher, "get a bigger engine."

"Yeahhhh," they all agreed.

Rick steered the boat towards Doe Bay Café's dock. As soon as he reached the dock, Greg jumped onto the dock. Quickly, Topher handed him the line. Within seconds the boat had a line secured to the dock and they and Aaron were jumping out of the boat.

"Man, I am getting hungry," said Greg as he walked up to the café. "I can smell those crab cakes already."

"Mrs. Hamilton makes the best crab cakes anywhere on the islands or mainland for that matter," added Topher.

Aaron gave two barks as if to say he agreed. Mrs. Hamilton always had a bowl of water set out and a special crab cake or two for him. He made it up to the café ahead of the boys.

"Well, my special boy is here today," commented Mrs. Hamilton with a smile to Aaron.

Aaron had let himself into the café and headed for the kitchen. He knew where he could find Mrs. Hamilton and her delicious crab cakes.

"I saw you and the boys coming around the point. So I have your lunch and water waiting for you by your special spot outside," she said as she opened the door. Aaron headed for the patio and to his dining area.

The boys passed Aaron as he came out of the café. Rick said to Aaron, "Boy Aaron, you are one lucky dog."

Upon hearing the boys come in, Mrs. Hamilton called out to them and said, "Your crab cakes are just coming out of the fryer. I take it you want fries and a milkshake too?"

"Yes ma'am," they replied.

The boys had been coming into the Doe Bay Café for years and they always ordered the same thing. Mrs. Hamilton always put a brownie on their plates and said it was to give them energy.

Greg looked around the café and asked, "Mrs. Hamilton is Mr. Hamilton around? Rick, Topher, and I would like to talk to him about a business proposition."

Mrs. Hamilton already knew what they were going to ask Mr. Hamilton and smiled as she said, "Yes, he should be back in about ten minutes. I will let him know when he gets back that you want to talk to him."

"OK, great," replied Greg.

The boys took their food outside to the patio and joined Aaron. Aaron was already done eating and circled the table where the boys were sitting. He was hoping for any cast off food they were willing to toss to him.

"Aaron go deep," said Rick as he tossed him a fry.

Mr. Hamilton had returned back to the café when he was told the boys wanted to talk to him.

"Hello mates," yelled Mr. Hamilton with his usual booming tone to the boys as he walked over to them.

"Hi Mr. Hamilton," they all said.

"I understand you boys might have a business proposition for me," he continued with a chuckle.

He pulled up a seat at their table. Aaron walked over to Mr. Hamilton, so he could get that great ear rub. Mr. Hamilton had a gruff exterior, but he was a real softy when it came to Aaron and the boys.

"Yes, we would like to supply your café with crabs this summer," said Topher. "Our boat is running well and we know of some great spots to catch them."

They looked up eagerly at Mr. Hamilton.

"You are good boys and I know I can count on you," he confidently replied. "So that is a YES!"

He must have known the boys were going to be asking because he had already figured out what he was going to pay them. "I want you boys to make a fair pay. You have to pay for gas and still have money left in your pockets. I have the crab pots and bait that you can use. I have extra buoy markers and you can write your names and address on them. Then folks will know they are your crab pots and leave them alone."

The boys were familiar with crab pots. Crab pots are made out of wire mesh and are typically in the shape of a cylinder. Inside the center of the crab pots is where the bait is placed. All crab pots must be equipped with a rot cord that rots away to allow the crab to escape freely if the pot is lost or abandoned.

The boys were excited. It was a lot more money than they had thought they would get. Mr. Hamilton saw how excited the boys were and was smiling.

"Oh, one more thing," he added "since you are working for me, you get a free lunch whenever you come to the café."

"Oh wow, this gets better and better," Rick said excitedly. "But, when we start to make money we will want to pay for our lunches."

Mr. Hamilton smiled at Rick's comment and

thought that was exactly what his own son would have said. Mr. & Mrs. Hamilton had only one son who was killed in a tragic accident many years ago and they had always had a soft spot for Greg, Rick, and Topher. When the boys were little, they would always come and visit the Hamiltons. Sometimes they would ride their bikes to the post office to pick up packages or mail for them. The Hamiltons were like their surrogate grandparents.

"Thanks Mrs. Hamilton, the lunch was great!" shouted the boys as they headed out the door.

Then to Mr. Hamilton they said, "As soon as we catch something, we will bring it by."

Mrs. Hamilton shouted back, "If you boys need anything you let us know. We aren't that far away."

Greg went over to the little country store that was next to the Doe Bay Café and bought another package of chocolate bars. Topher and Rick went down to their boat to load the crab pots and bait into the boat. When they were just about ready to set sail, Captain MacArthur, of the Coast Guard, was pulling into the docks. Topher and Greg ran over to give him a hand with his lines. Captain MacArthur was Matt and Thomas' uncle. The boys knew Captain MacArthur very well and had taken their Coast Guard boating class from him.

"Hey Captain!" yelled Topher.

"Hey guys, how are you doing?" answered Captain MacArthur. "Boy, it didn't take you boys long to make it over here for Mrs. Hamilton's crab cakes. I heard you came over yesterday afternoon from the mainland."

"Yes sir," said Greg.

"By the look of things, it looks like you boys have

a job getting crabs for the Hamiltons," commented Captain MacArthur as he pointed to the crab pots in their boat.

"Yes sir," said Rick. "We are going to be working very hard too."

Captain MacArthur smiled and continued, "Have you boys seen anything strange going on since you arrived?" He looked at them carefully.

The boys looked at each other and instantly had the same understanding on how to reply.

Quickly, Topher answered him, "No, we haven't seen anything out of the ordinary. Why?"

"Oh, I just heard there might be some troublemakers in the area causing problems," he answered and then added, "Well, if you see anything unusual, let me know."

"Yes Captain, we will," said Greg.

Captain MacArthur headed up to the Doe Bay Café. He, like everyone else in the area, never wasted any time getting those tasty crab cakes and warm greeting from the Hamiltons.

As soon as the boys set sail, Topher said over the noise of the motor, "See, I told you it was Matt and Thomas messing around with us. Why else would the Captain ask us if we saw anything strange going on?"

"Troublemakers in the area," said Greg and then continuing, "The only troublemakers in the area are Matt and Thomas."

Topher and Rick agreed with him.

"Aarh, aarh," barked the seals that were sitting on the channel markers just outside the bay in the water. As the boys motored past the seals, Aaron just sat in the boat looking at them and didn't answer back. He didn't pay attention to them at all.

Greg was surprised at Aaron's lack of interest in them and said, "Aaron, aren't you going to say anything to them?"

Aaron just wagged his tail and walked over to Greg for an ear rub.

"Boy, you were having a fit with them yesterday. Today, you could care less," added Rick.

Then all of a sudden, Aaron started to act agitated and paced around in the boat. He hung his head down, but instead of barking like he did the other day, his tail was wagging very fast just like he does when he sees the boys.

Then suddenly, W - O – O – S – H --- something swam very quickly under their boat. As the boys looked out over the bow of the boat they could see it was below the surface and moving very fast. It was moving faster than a seal could move.

"OK, what was that?" shouted Rick.

"Wow, that was just like what happened yesterday," exclaimed Greg.

"Did you notice that Aaron didn't get upset this time?" said Topher in a puzzled tone. "He knew something was coming, but just wagged his tail. Do you think it was a seal?"

"Boy, I don't know," said Greg with his voice trailing off.

They shook their heads in complete wonderment. It was a few minutes before any of them spoke. They kept trying to make sense of whatever it was that kept swimming under and past their boat quickly.

"How fast do you think it was going?" asked Rick.

"Well, we are going fast at about 18 knots and whatever it was flew past us like we were standing still," deduced Greg.

Topher added, "I don't know of any sea animal that can move that fast!"

Rick said, "I am going to ask my dad when he comes out this weekend if he knows of any sea animal that can move that fast. He may know."

"Once we get to the docks, I will go to my cabin and get my handheld GPS, Global Positioning System, device," said Greg. "Then tomorrow, we can set out the crab pots and mark their exact locations on the map. We can keep track of the areas that are bringing in the crabs. I have the locations of a few spots where I caught a lot of crabs last year written down in my notebook and we can try them this year."

The boys understood the benefits of using a GPS device and knew how to use it.

Topher and Rick thought it was a great idea. The boys were putting together their plans to catch the most crabs as they could.

They went to bed early that night because they wanted to get an early start the next morning. Aaron wanted to go outside, but the boys told him to settle down because they had a long day planned for tomorrow. They must have checked the doors in the cabin two or three times to make sure everything was locked. They looked outside to see if they saw the lights again from the cliff, but the cliff area was dark.

Although they were enjoying their freedom, they were also excited their parents were coming out the next day. They agreed they were not going to tell their parents about the strange events with the lights and the tracks by the beach and the cabin. They were concerned that if they told their parents that perhaps they wouldn't let them stay out on the island by themselves. Also, deep down they kept hoping it was Matt and Thomas playing tricks on them. If they said something and it was just Matt and Thomas, then their parents might think they weren't ready to stay out on the island during the week.

During the night, whenever Aaron woke up and walked around the dormitory, the boys would look around to see if anyone was looking into their window. Any little creak or sound would wake them up. At first, it seemed like they would never get to sleep, but finally after becoming exhausted, they fell fast asleep.

Chapter 3

The boys woke up before dawn. They quickly ate their breakfast, which was a bowl of cereal and a glass of milk. Rick reached into the refrigerator and grabbed the crab bait. The best thing to catch crabs with is chicken parts. Mrs. Hamilton would always save the unwanted bits and pieces of the chicken parts from her café's kitchen for the crab pots. Rick loaded up the cooler with the chicken pieces while Greg got his GPS device. Topher got a pencil, paper, and marine charts to mark the coordinates down.

Aaron ran ahead down to the boat and waited for Rick to put his life jacket on him. After the boys put their life jackets on, they jumped into the boat and started the engine. Rick released the lines from the dock cleat and the boys were off.

The sun was coming up over the water when the boys lowered their first crab pot down into the water. Greg read off the coordinates from his GPS device and Topher wrote them down.

Then, Greg said, "OK, we need to head north and east a little more and we can place the next pot down."

Rick steered the boat over to where Greg had recommended and Topher lowered the next crab pot down. They continued placing the rest of the crab pots down in the water. All the locations were carefully recorded.

"How long should we wait before checking the pots to see what we have caught?" asked Rick.

The boys were eager to see how many crabs they could catch and how long it would take.

"Let's come out this afternoon and check the pots," answered Greg. "Hopefully, we will have caught some by then."

As they looked out onto the water, they saw other crabbers dropping their pots into the water. Everyone had their own markers and special spots where they liked to drop their pots. Everyone knew whose pots were dropped down by the names on the buoy markers that floated on the water. The buoy markers were used to mark the location of the crab pots and that was how the crabbers knew where to recover their pots. The boys recognized most of the crabbers and gave them a wave when they passed them.

After the last crab pot was dropped into the water, the boys headed back to their dock. Their parents were coming out later that afternoon and they wanted to make sure the cabin was straightened up. The boys washed their dishes, made their beds, and picked up their swim suits from the floor.

"Topher and I are going to take our gear over to our cabins, open up the cabin windows, and go through our to-do lists before our parents arrive tonight," said Greg to Rick.

The boys had a list of chores their parents had left for them to do. They wanted to show their parents they were responsible, so they checked off their lists to make sure they had completed everything they were asked to do. The boys thought they should do their chores in the morning while they were waiting on the crab pots to hopefully fill with crabs.

As the boys went off to do their chores, Aaron, with his nose to the ground, went running off to the cliff. He had his own to-do list.

"Let's plan to meet back at the docks by 11:30," yelled Rick as Topher and Greg headed out the door.

"OK, sounds good," they replied.

At 11:30 with their chores completed the boys met at the dock. Aaron with his tail wagging was back from his run in the woods.

They boarded the boat, started the engine, and headed off to their first buoy. Greg reached down and grabbed the buoy.

"Wow, this feels heavy. I hope we caught a lot of crabs and ones that we can keep," said Greg as he pulled on the line that was connected to the crab pot at the bottom of the sea.

The boys knew all the rules of crabbing. They had

their Catch Record Card (CRC) with them. They knew the three Ss of crabbing, which stood for Season, Sex, and Size. Greg had his crab gauge, which was used to

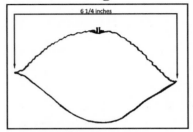

measure the size of the crab. In order for the boys to keep the crab, it has to measure no smaller than 6 ¼ inches across the carapace inside the tips.

Also, the crab has to be a male. Females are put back into the water, so they can breed. The boys turned the crabs over and they could tell if the crab was male because they have a narrow abdominal flap, whereas the females have a wide abdominal flap.

Female Abdominal Flap

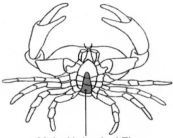

Male Abdominal Flap

Lastly, it had to be the correct season. The shells had to be hard. If it had a soft shell that meant that it could still produce crabs. They needed to leave them in the water, so the crab population would be replenished.

As he pulled the crab pot up, Rick whistled and said, "Wow, there are a lot of crabs in the pot. I hope most of them are keepers."

Topher said, "It looks like most of them are keepers. Maybe only two of them have to go back."

"Yeah, we did great on this catch," confirmed Greg. "I can hardly wait to check the rest of the pots."

The boys went around to all of their pots and had the same results. Eagerly they pulled up the pots and returned those crabs to the sea they could not keep.

"Let's get them over to Mr. Hamilton. I think he is going to be impressed with our catch," Greg and Topher said almost in unison.

Rick agreed and they proudly set sail for the Doe Bay Café. The boys had recorded their catch and properly stored the crabs for transport to the Doe Bay Café.

When they arrived at the Doe Bay Café dock, they were very excited to show Mr. Hamilton their catch. After securing their boat onto the dock, Greg and Rick loaded the cooler of crabs on the dock while Topher held the boat to the dock. They didn't want to drop the cooler into the water. Aaron jumped onto the dock and started heading off to see Mrs. Hamilton. His tail was wagging as he could feel the excitement from the boys.

Greg and Rick carried the cooler up to the side door of the café near the kitchen. Mr. Hamilton had seen the boys arrive and could tell by the way they were carrying their cooler they had a great catch.

"Hey there mates, looks like you had a good catch!" said Mr. Hamilton enthusiastically.

"Yes sir!" answered the boys with even more enthusiasm.

As soon as they reached Mr. Hamilton, they opened up the cooler. They were smiling from ear to ear. Aaron stuck his nose into the cooler as if he were counting the crabs and then sat back very pleased.

"You boys did a fantastic job," exclaimed Mr. Hamilton. "Now, you know that you won't always be this lucky. Also, if anyone asks how you did, just say you did well, but hope to do better. You don't want to give your prime spots away. Sometimes, mates that brag lose their prime crabbing spots to someone else."

The boys understood what Mr. Hamilton was saying. They had been around fishermen and knew how they were when they talked about their catches. They also didn't want to give away their prime spots. Although they understood they wouldn't always do this well, they hoped that they would.

"Let's take them inside and Mrs. Hamilton can prepare them," said Mr. Hamilton as he opened the door for the boys to carry the cooler into the kitchen. "Myrtle, you should see how many crabs the boys caught on their first day," said Mr. Hamilton.

Mrs. Hamilton looked into the cooler and said, "Wow, you boys have to be excited. It looks like I have my work cut out for me. With this many crabs, I can make a special dish of crab legs tonight!"

Mr. Hamilton told the boys to come into his office. The boys walked into his office and it smelled like a mixture of crab cakes and pipe tobacco. The boys never saw him smoke his pipe, but they knew he used to smoke his pipe late in the evening when Mrs. Hamilton was not around. He gave the boys their pay and they were excited. They quickly started to divide the money between themselves. They put half of the money into one envelope marked "Greg, Rick, and Topher." The money in this envelope was going to be saved by all of them. It was going to be used, as they would decide, at some future time. The other half was split equally between the three of them.

Mr. Hamilton saw the boys set aside half of their pay and asked, "What are you setting that aside for?"

Rick replied with a smile, "We aren't sure yet, we have a lot of ideas though. We might have it figured out by the end of summer."

Greg and Topher nodded their heads in agreement.

"You mates are smart," acknowledged Mr. Hamilton. "A lot of mates just spend it as they get it. Then, they wonder where it all went. Yes sir, you mates are smart," he said again with a nod.

The boys were proud of their choice to save half of their income from crabbing.

"What are you mates up to next?" asked Mr. Hamilton.

Greg replied, "We are going to go over to the Sweet Treat Bakery and get cinnamon rolls for our families. They are coming out this afternoon and we thought they might like the treat."

Mr. Hamilton smiled and said, "Good thinkin' mates. They'll be happy you thought of them."

Aaron had been outside running around smelling everything. It seemed like every blade of grass was getting marked the way male dogs liked to do. When Aaron saw the boys head off towards the bakery, he quickly joined them. The sweet smell of fresh baked goods filled the air outside the Sweet Treat Bakery. As they opened the door to the bakery, the bell on the door clanged against the door. Within seconds, Mrs. Sweet was walking into the front of the bakery carrying a pan of fresh baked peanut butter cookies. The boys were busy studying all the wonderful treats in the display case. Aaron was left outside by accident, but within a few tries he had the door open and was trotting inside.

Topher looked back as he heard the bell clang against the door and said, "Sorry boy. I thought you were right behind me. I was a little distracted by all the wonderful goodies."

"Hey, Mrs. Sweet," said Rick. "Boy everything looks and smells wonderful."

As she was placing the cookies carefully in the display, she reached in and took out a few cookies and said, "Here is a peanut butter cookie for each of you." She gave them each a cookie. Aaron sat very patiently as she tossed him one too. Quickly the peanut butter cookies were eaten by the boys. "What do you think of my new peanut butter cookie? I am adding a little more peanut butter in my recipe and of course a secret ingredient."

With mouths full they replied, "Hmmm, great!"

"What can I get for you boys?" she asked.

They looked carefully at the prices and Greg said, "I'll take six large cinnamon rolls."

Rick had a weakness for chocolate, so he ordered six cinnamon rolls and four double chocolate chip cookies. Topher and his mom liked the double chocolate chip brownies and so he ordered four of them and two peanut butter cookies for the trip back to the cabin.

"Wow, I still have a lot of money left over even after buying the sweets," stated Topher.

"It sure feels good to have extra spending money in my pocket," added Rick.

Topher and Greg agreed with Rick.

Feeling very satisfied with the business of the day, the boys got into their boat and headed back to the cabin. They were no sooner docked and had carried the sweets up to their cabins when they heard the engines of their parents' boats arriving. They ran down to the docks and helped with their lines.

"Thanks Topher," said his mom, Mrs. Susan Aldrich, as he took the line and then helped her out of the boat.

She had come over with Rick's parents, Rick and Anna Taylor, and Rick's little sister, Regina. Greg's parents, Jason and Terri Ebert, and his older sister, Mary, were just arriving in their boat. The boys' parents had known each other all throughout their childhood.

As soon as the boys' families unloaded their groceries and gear on the dock, they made plans to get together for a bonfire that night.

The boys were eager to share their good news of their catch earlier that day with their families and get caught up on family news. After hearing the boys' news, the parents had told the boys how proud they were of their efforts and happy for their success. When they went into their cabins, they were impressed at how neat everything was and also that the boys thought to buy breakfast treats for their families. The boys were definitely scoring great points for maturity from their parents.

It was a great weekend for the boys and their families. The boys had not realized how much they had missed their parents and siblings.

Every evening when they sat outside with their families, the boys would look up at the cliff to see if they saw any lights flashing.

"I keep looking up at the cliff since our parents have arrived and I haven't seen anything," commented Rick quietly to Topher and Greg.

"I have been looking around for any signs of those strange tracks and I haven't seen any new ones either," added Topher.

"That certainly proves that it probably is Matt and Thomas. They wouldn't want to do it while our folks are here. Also, their parents are probably out on the island this weekend keeping a close eye on them," asserted Greg.

The boys all nodded in agreement.

Late in the afternoon, the boys' families were getting ready to go back to the mainland. The boys were sad to see them leaving, but were excited to start catching crabs and earning money.

Everyone met down at the docks and was loading up their gear in their boats.

"Topher, be careful when you are out on the water," warned Susan to her son.

"Don't worry, Mom. We always wear our life jackets and are careful," answered Topher.

"Greg, make sure you put sunscreen on. You know how easily you burn," said Terri.

As the moms shared all their reminders with

the boys, they nodded their heads answered back respectfully that they would --- be careful, wear sunscreen, call them if they had any problems, not eat too many sweets, not to stay up too late, and the list went on. They knew their moms were concerned over their health and safety.

Then, Rick's mom said something that surprised the boys, "Well, I am sure you boys may get a little bored since Matt and Thomas won't be coming to the island for at least two weeks. I know the boys always provide entertainment with their antics."

The boys looked at each other in a state of shock. Then Rick recovered and asked, "When did they leave the island?"

"They haven't been to the island since last month," said Anna. "Their grandmother had surgery and their mom and the boys went to Eastern Washington to help take care of her as she recovers."

"Are you sure they haven't been out here, Mrs. Taylor?" asked Topher.

"Yes," she replied and then continued, "I took over a few nursing care supplies that I have. Why do you ask?"

"Oh, nothing, we just thought we saw them on the island this past week. It probably was someone else or our imaginations. You know we always expect to see them," stated Topher.

The boys kept looking back at each other and were beginning to get a little concerned. The shocked look on their faces was starting to get a little hard to hide.

Then Rick's mom leaned into the boys and

whispered something that really shocked them!

Anna whispered, "Don't worry boys, I went into the dormitory this morning and saw your little project. I put it in the dormitory closet, so no one else would see it." And then she continued as the boys stood there with their mouths open in complete shock, "He is very cute and almost seems life-like. Aaron and he were playing together in the dormitory. I tried to turn his switch off, but couldn't find it." Then with a laugh and a smiling glance continued, "I even looked under its tail to see if the off and on switch was there. I know how silly you boys can be. But, then it turned off. Aaron must have been playing with it and accidently turned it on."

Aaron had heard his name being mentioned and ran up to the boys on the dock. Rick put his hand down on his dog and rubbed is ears. He looked at him and wished he could talk, because Aaron would have a lot to tell them.

Since Rick didn't know what his mom was talking about, he stammered in reply, "Ahhhh, geee, thanks --- Mom."

"Yeahhh, great, good thinking Mrs. Taylor," said Greg equally as slow to respond.

Topher just made an inaudible sound because no sound would come out.

Anna Taylor just looked at the boys and smiled. She thought it was cute to see what they were making and how they were surprised she had seen it.

The boys stood stunned on the dock and waved to there families as they set sail. They stood there waving almost mechanically because they were still in shock.

As they stood their waving, they all thought the same thing – I need to run as fast as I can to the dormitory and see what it is.

As soon as their families rounded the corner, Topher was the first to recover his voice and all he could say was, "Quick! Dormitory!"

Without hesitating a second, they started to run towards the cabin and up to the dormitory. They were almost tripping from running very fast. Aaron, seeing where they were headed, ran up in front with his tail wagging and barking as if to say, "Hey guys, hurry up!"

Their hearts were bounding when they all fell into the dormitory. The closet door was shut. Aaron went over to the door and started to paw at the door. Since Aaron could open just about any door, he had the door open within a few tries. The door banged open and Aaron trotted in. He started barking and the boys stood frozen in fear.

"You go. No, you go," they kept saying to each other. Neither of them wanted to go inside the closet to see what it was.

"Maybe, your mom just got us something and wanted to surprise us," said Topher to Rick.

"Yeah," said Greg. "She might have thought that we needed something to do when we weren't crabbing."

"Maybe?" replied Rick in the form of a question.

Aaron barked again and then what the boys saw coming out of the closet almost made them faint.

Chapter 4

As the boys fixed their gaze on the closet door, time seemed to be moving in slow motion. Aaron walked out of the closet with a ROBOTIC DOG walking next to him. The robot dog matched Aaron's gait, so that when Aaron stopped, it stopped. The robot dog was approximately the same height as Aaron. It had short ears that stood straight up like a Doberman Pinscher and a long tail about the same length as Aaron's. The robot dog did not have fur, but was made out of a metal or some kind of plastic.

Aaron walked towards the boys and sat down. The boys sat down on the floor in the dormitory as Aaron and the robot dog approached them. The robot dog kept pace with Aaron and sat down next to him. Aaron looked over at the robot dog and the robot dog looked at him. Aaron licked the robot dog on the face and the robot dog licked him back. Then, Aaron's tail thumped and wagged on the floor and the robot dog's tail did exactly the same thing. It was like the robot dog was mimicking Aaron's every action.

It seemed like a very long time before the boys recovered their voices.

Rick spoke first, "Guys, what in the world is it?"

Topher replied, "It looks like a robotic dog."

"I think it is just mimicking Aaron's actions, but it looks and acts real," added Greg.

When Greg was talking, the robot dog turned his head towards Greg. It appeared as if he was listening to Greg.

Aaron barked and then the robot dog barked. The sound that came from the robot dog sounded a little mechanical.

The boys laughed a little at the humor of it and a little bit from feeling tense from the strange encounter.

Rick jokingly said to the robot dog, "Hello."

The robot dog answered back, "Hello."

"That is cool," said Greg.

Then Greg said to the robot dog, "What is your name?"

The dog answered back, "What is your name?"

The boys were enjoying it and still believed it was a toy.

Then, Greg answered, "My name is Greg."

The boys thought for sure the robot dog was going to say the same thing. They were laughing and anticipating that the robot dog was going to say, "My name is Greg."

However, what the dog did say was, "My name is Markarian 818."

"Whoa! Did you hear that?" asked Topher.

The boys just sat looking at the robot dog. They were stunned by his responses.

"OK, this is weird," said Rick.

"It must be programed to say certain things," reasoned Greg.

"Yeah, that's it," said Topher.

Each time the boys would speak, the robot dog would turn his face towards whomever was speaking.

"It looks like he was programmed to follow voices," said Topher.

Then the robot dog looked at Topher and said, "What is your name?"

Topher replied, "Topher."

Then the robot dog looked at Rick and without asking his name, Rick said to the dog, "Rick." Rick continued by speaking to Topher and Greg, "What? He looked at me and wanted me to say my name."

While holding their sides, the boys began to laugh very hard. Next, Rick got on all fours and crawled over to the robotic dog and sat down next to him in the same way the dogs were sitting. Rick turned his head in a mechanical way like the robot dog did, looked at him, and then the boys. The boys were roaring with laughter at this point and then Rick said, "Hello, my name is Markarian 818."

The robot dog turned his head like Rick did when

he was mimicking the robot dog and said, "No, I am Markarian 818. You are Rick!"

Next, the robot dog looked at each boy and said, "Hello Rick, Topher, Greg." Then he turned to Aaron and said, "Hello Bark!"

By now, the boys were laughing even harder and began to roll on the floor.

Aaron started to scratch his ear with his hind leg and suddenly the robot dog did the same thing.

Greg said through hysterical laughter, "Oh my gosh, that is so funny. Look, he is scratching his ear like Aaron."

Topher said, "Let's call him Markie." To the robot dog he said, "Can we call you Markie for short?"

The robot dog moved his head around and looked at the boys and said, "Yes, Topher. You can call me Markie."

Topher looked at the boys and said, "Wow, I didn't expect him to say that. I thought he was going to say his name was Markarian 818."

"Let's ask him questions and see how he is programmed to respond," said Rick. Then he asked, "How did you get here?"

"I got here in my Intergalactic Transporter," answered Markie.

To Markie, Greg said, "We got here in our Intergalactic Transporter too."

Markie looked at each of the boys and said, "No, you came in your boat."

"OK, now this is starting to get weird," commented Topher.

"Oh, my gosh I didn't think of it, but maybe my mom put Markie here to keep an eye on us like a Nanny Cam," reasoned Rick. "She is probably watching us right now and answering us through a voice transmitter."

Greg whispered in Rick's ear, "Say you are going outside to check on something. Then, call your mom and dad on your cell phone and keep them busy on the phone. Topher and I will ask Markie some questions."

Rick answered back softly, "OK, great idea."

"I will be right back in a minute," said Rick as he got up and left the room with his cell phone.

While Rick was talking to his mom and dad on his cell phone, Greg and Topher were asking Markie questions about his Intergalactic Transporter. After talking to his parents, Rick went back upstairs and said, "Well, did Markie stop talking?"

Both boys shook their head No and then Topher said, "Markie has been busy telling us about his Intergalactic Transporter."

In shock, Rick muttered, "What?"

"Uh – huh," replied Topher.

Markie looked at Rick and then at Greg and Topher as if he was trying to understand their odd expressions.

"I am beginning to think that Markie is NOT a toy," said Greg. "You wouldn't believe what he has been telling us. When we asked him questions, he answered us with a lot of detail."

Topher added, "There is just no way that he is a toy. I have never seen or heard anything like it."

Rick said, "What else has he said?"

The boys then started to tell Rick what they had

learned about Markie – Markie was traveling in his Intergalactic Transporter to a different galaxy than his own when his transporter was hit by an unexpected electrical charge. It sent his transporter traveling out of control. Next, he found he was in our galaxy and closing in on Earth. As his transporter was approaching the water, he ejected. After that, his transporter crashed somewhere into the Puget Sound. He said that his circuits were badly damaged and all he remembers is floating on the water for an unknown amount time. While floating in the ocean, he shut down some of his functions, so that he could try to repair himself.

Then finally, he washed up onto the Orcas Island shoreline. Not knowing who or what was on the planet, he went up to the cliff across from our cove and tried to complete the repairs to his circuits the best that he could.

Topher and Greg looked at Rick who sat there trying to take in everything he was hearing about Markie and how he got to Orcas Island. What Rick was hearing didn't seem real. The boys were beginning to feel like they were dreaming all of this.

After he composed himself, Rick asked, "Was that you flashing your lights at us the other night?"

Markie answered, "Yes, I saw you flash your light at me and I answered your signal."

"What signal?" asked Greg.

"The Morse code signals you sent me. At first I did not understand how you were trying to communicate, but when I accessed my Internal Knowledge Unit (IKU), I reasoned that flashing lights could be a Morse code signal. However, your flashing lights did not match up with any letters in Morse code. So I tried using a red light for the dots and a green light for the dashes, but when you flashed back it did not make sense."

"I have heard of Morse code," said Rick, "but I don't know how to do it. Good thing I didn't accidently send the wrong signal that you might have misinterpreted."

"Phew, I am glad that was you. We didn't know who it was," said Topher.

"What is your Internal Knowledge Unit?" asked Greg.

"My IKU is where all of my functions and knowledge are stored. I have the ability to access information either through your internet or individual computers. Your internet is very slow compared to how we send data in the Markarian Galaxy. To access the internet on Earth, I use your satellites that are orbiting Earth or your cellular networks. The signals bounce back the information to my Internal Knowledge Unit. After I receive the information, I review it and synthesize it in my Internal Knowledge Unit," stated Markie.

Then Greg looked down at Markie's legs and said to Rick and Topher, "Look at his paws! They have the outline of the tracks we saw in the sand along the beach and by the house."

"Yeah, you're right," confirmed Topher.

As Rick pointed to the dormitory window he asked, "Were you looking into that window the other night?"

"Yes, I have leg extensions and I can extend myself," replied Markie. "I have many different kinds of functions I can perform. I wanted to learn additional information about you, Greg, Topher, and Bark, so I looked into your window."

"Bark? ---- Oh, you mean Aaron. His name is Aaron," said Rick as he pointed to Aaron.

"Oh, Aaron, OK," said Markie. "When I saw Aaron he said he would come and visit me the next morning."

"Well, that explains why Aaron has been running off into the woods," said Greg.

"Is anyone else with you?" asked Topher.

"No, I came here alone. I was not planning on coming to this galaxy or planet Earth," answered Markie sadly.

"Markie, where is your transporter?" asked Rick.

Markie looked at Rick and said, "I am not sure. I have been swimming under the water trying to find it. I was badly damaged when I crashed into the ocean. I can't recall the crash location. My Internal Imaging Unit was damaged on impact."

Topher questioned Markie about his Internal Imaging Unit. Markie explained his eyes are like lenses of a camera. They are used to capture images of objects or scenes in three-dimensions. When he wants to show someone the images, he can bring the images up on his chest plate screen. The images can be zoomed in or out and enhanced to be either sharper, lighter, or darker. His Internal Knowledge Unit filters the information and decides what is important to store for access at a later time.

"Boy, I wish I had one of those Internal Imaging Units when I go to take a test at school," laughed Topher.

"Yours is called your memory," replied Markie.

"Well, let's just say my Internal Memory Unit gets damaged each time I walk through the school's force field," jokingly replied Topher.

Rick and Greg laughed and shook their heads yes with that comment, but Markie just had a quizzical look at his comment.

Markie said, "I will need to investigate this force field at your school."

"What galaxy are you from?" inquired Greg.

"I am from the Markarian Galaxy. Look at the screen on my chest plate and I will show you an image of my galaxy.

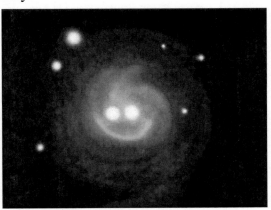

The Markarian Galaxy

"No way, that just looks like a smiley face. OK, now I am back to thinking this is a joke," said Rick.

"Look it up on the information source you call the internet," commanded Markie.

The boys walked over to Rick's computer and looked it up.

"No way, no way, way cool," they kept muttering as they read about the Markarian Galaxy.

They read the Markarian Galaxy resembles a smiley face because it has a pair of bright cores that are underscored by an arcing spiral arm. It is actually a pair of merging galaxies. The two super massive black holes are separated by about 11,000 light-years. The Markarian Galaxy is 425 million light-years away from the constellation Leo.

The boys were mesmerized by the information they found while researching the Markarian Galaxy. They went to the National Aeronautics and Space Administration's (NASA's) website to read additional information.

After reading the basic information about the Markarian Galaxy, they began to bombard Markie with a ton of questions about his galaxy and home planet.

Markie was happy to share the information about his galaxy with the boys. He was glad they were interested. It was just the beginning of many more questions the boys would ask Markie about his galaxy and planet.

The boys realized there were many things they had yet to learn about Markie and what he was capable of doing.

Suddenly, Topher asked, "Was that you swimming under our boat the other day?"

"Yes, I have been searching for my transporter and I haven't found it yet."

The boys were glad to hear that it was Markie swimming under their boat.

"Do you think Captain MacArthur saw Markie and

thought it was someone causing problems in the area?" asked Rick. He then continued speaking to Markie, "Do you think anyone else has seen you? Or, have you talked to anyone else?"

"Rick's mom saw me, but she thought I was a toy that you had built. I don't think anyone else has seen me nor have I talked to anyone else, but you, Greg, Topher, and Aaron," he replied. "Let me access my Internal Imaging Unit to make sure."

Markie quickly checked his Internal Imaging Unit and then said with certainty, "No one else has seen me. Why do you ask?"

"Well, Captain MacArthur had told us there are troublemakers in the area. I was thinking maybe someone saw the ripple in the water that you were making, like we did, and thought it was someone causing problems," answered Rick.

"So if it isn't Markie," said Greg, "then who was the Captain talking about?"

"We will have to ask him when we see him again," asserted Topher.

They agreed and then Greg said, "You know, we shouldn't tell anyone about Markie. If people find out about him, they will take him away and do experiments on him or something."

"Yeah," they all chimed in.

"I don't want to be taken away!" exclaimed Markie. "I need to find my transporter and go home."

"Don't worry, Markie," assured Rick. "We won't let anyone take you away and no one will ever suspect you are from another galaxy."

"But, your mom has already seen him," said Greg.

"Yes, but she thinks he is a toy we built," confirmed Rick.

"Right," exclaimed Topher, "so that is the perfect cover. His real identity can be hidden in plain sight!"

Everyone agreed it was the best plan to hide Markie in plain sight.

"We can introduce him slowly. The next time our families come out to the island, we will show them Markie. We will say we have been busy programming him and soon he will almost seem life-like," stated Topher.

Greg said to Markie, "When you are around our families, just pretend you are a toy that Rick, Topher, and I have built."

"OK," agreed Markie. "I can answer questions with a simple response. Then, when they try to turn me off, I will go still like I did when your mom tried to turn me off."

"Great idea," said the boys.

"Where do you stay at night?" asked Rick.

"Alone on the cliff in the woods," answered Markie.

The boys looked at each other and nodded their heads. They each knew what they were all thinking and Rick said, "Markie, you can stay here at my house with us all the time if you want to. Then you won't be alone."

"Great! I will," said Markie and then he smiled.

Aaron hearing all the happy voices turned and gave Markie a lick. Markie turned and licked Aaron.

Markie, Aaron, and the boys had a plan and they were excited.

Markie had stayed hidden from everyone since he had arrived on Earth. He reasoned it might not be safe to expose his presence to just anyone. However, when he observed the boys and Aaron, he decided they were friendly and would not harm him. He was beginning to realize how right he was. He also thought about how long he could be stranded on Earth before he could return home. He was glad he had the friendship of the boys and Aaron.

"Markie, are there any people like us in your galaxy?" asked Greg.

Markie answered, "No, we are what you call robots. We have different shapes and sizes. We have something similar to families in our galaxy. My family looks similar to my shape and Aaron's."

Then all of a sudden, Aaron started to scratch his ear and Markie did the same thing.

"Markie, why do you scratch and lick like Aaron does when you see him doing it?" asked Topher.

Markie answered, "I mimic certain behaviors, so I can blend in to my surroundings. Since my shape is that of a dog, I mimic what a dog would do. The other day when Aaron was in the woods, he lifted his rear leg and leaked a liquid onto the vegetation. I walked up behind him and did the same thing. Then, he came back and smelled it again and leaked more liquid. We kept repeating it over and over, but you called him and he left."

The boys started to laugh at thought of the two of them doing that over and over again.

Markarian 818

RECEIVE SIGNAL

LED EYES!

ON SCREEN

Aarf!

OFF!

8 Feet

TAIL WITH LED!

FINGER EXTENSIONS

Chapter 5

"Wow, it is getting late. We should go and lay our crab pots down," suggested Topher.

"Markie, if you want to come with us, you can," said Greg. "We are going to put crab pots out, so we can catch crabs. We are earning money by selling the crabs we catch to Mr. Hamilton. He and his wife own the Doe Bay Café."

"There is a lot I need to learn about your life on Earth," said Markie. "I keep constantly accessing my Internal Knowledge Unit to understand what you are telling me."

"Well, if we went to your galaxy, we would be very confused. We are still learning about Earth and many things still confuse us as well," commented Rick with a grin.

"I'll get the bait," said Greg as he reached into the refrigerator.

"Grab some pop too and a water bottle for Aaron," requested Rick. "Markie, do you drink anything?"

"I drink something similar to your drinking water, but I need a salinity of at least 3.5%," he answered. Then when he saw the confused looks on the boys' expressions he said, "You also call it seawater."

"Ohhhhhh," they responded while shaking their heads in acknowledgement.

Then Rick added, "Well, there is a lot of that in the bay."

Rick, Topher, Aaron, and Markie headed down to the docks and put on their life jackets. Greg was bringing the small cooler with the bait, pop, and water. They looked at Markie, but after remembering how well he swam in the water, they agreed he didn't need a life jacket.

Aaron jumped into the boat followed by Markie, Rick, and Topher. Greg handed the cooler to Rick, loosened the lines from the dock, and then jumped into the boat.

Rick set a course towards Lost Cove. It was near Lost Cove where they had caught a lot of crabs the other day. Greg was busy getting out his GPS, Global Positioning System, and his notebook before helping Topher with the bait. The boys always took turns doing the different jobs.

Markie sat and watched as Greg and Topher took the bait out of the cooler and put it in each of the crab pots. They explained to him how the crabs are attracted to the bait and crawl into the crab pots. The crabs are then prevented from escaping the crab pots until the boys return to either keep them or release them back into the sea. They told Markie it can take many hours before the crabs become attracted to the bait in the crab pots. They drop the crab pots down and then return later to pull the crab pots up out of the water to see if they caught any crabs. If they do, then they decide if they can keep them by following the three Ss of crabbing.

Aaron started sniffing the crab pots and Markie began to smell the pots, too.

Markie commented, "There are a lot of interesting smells on these crab pots."

Aaron barked, "Yes," in agreement.

One by one, the boys dropped the crab pots down into the water. Greg looked at his GPS and Topher marked their coordinates down in the notebook.

Aaron hung his head down and watched as the pots were lowered. Markie did the same thing.

After a few pots had been lowered into the water, Greg took over steering the boat. Rick looked over the notes from the other day and said, "Greg take a heading of 345 degrees. I think that will take us over to the spot where we caught a lot of crabs the other day."

"OK," said Greg as he looked at the boat's compass and changed course.

As they approached the site Rick was talking about, they saw two red and white buoys bobbing in the water.

"Ah man, someone must have seen us pulling up a

lot of crabs the other day from this spot," said Topher.

Greg said, "I'll steer the boat close to the buoys and let's see if we can read the names on them. I want to know who saw us pulling up our crab pots the other day. Then in the future, we will be able to watch out for them when we are pulling up our pots."

"Good idea," agreed Topher and Rick.

"Wait, let's look around and make sure no one is watching us. I don't want to get into trouble," warned Rick.

"Yeah, it is a criminal offense to mess around with someone's buoys or crab pots," confirmed Topher.

The boys looked around the sea and decided no one was watching them.

Greg said, "Rick, look at the name on the buoy and Topher and I will be the lookouts."

Carefully, Rick took the telescoping boat hook from the side of their boat and hooked the buoy.

Rick read out the name, "Johhhhnnn_____. I can't make out the last name. The writing is kind of messed up. I think it starts with a G. Wait, it's G r a h a r – no wait it is an *m* not an *r* at the end. John Graham."

"Boy, I don't know anyone with that name," said Topher. "Do you guys know anyone with that name?"

"No," they answered.

Greg quickly said, "Look and see if you can read his address."

Again, Rick used the telescoping boat hook to try and turn the buoy around, so he could read the address. The address was smeared like the name and the buoy kept rolling around. Quickly, Markie jumped into the water. He swam over to the buoy and stopped for a second. Aaron's tail was wagging as he watched Markie swimming around. Aaron started to whimper and kept trying to jump into the water with Markie.

"Aaron, STAY!" commanded Rick. "What is Markie doing?"

"I don't know," said Greg.

Then, just as quickly as he jumped into the water, he swam back over to the boat and jumped back in.

Markie said, "Look at the screen on my chest plate. It will show you an image of the buoy."

The boys looked at his chest plate as he showed them the 3-D image of the buoy.

Markie said, "If you touch the screen on my chest plate, you can turn the image around and see all the sides."

"That is sooo cool," said Topher as he put his finger on the screen and moved the image around. "Thank you."

Markie was happy to help the boys even though he didn't understand why they were upset someone found their prime crabbing spot.

The boys were touching the screen on Markie's chest plate. Aaron, seeing the boys touch Markie's screen, rolled over on his back demanding he get a belly rub too. Aaron thought the boys were giving Markie a belly rub.

"OK boy, we will give you a belly rub," said Rick.

Topher said, "You are right, Rick. The name is John Graham. The address is badly smeared. I can't read the street address, but the name of the city looks like

Seattle."

The boys were now looking at Markie's screen and trying to decipher the writing on the buoy.

Rick said, "You know it almost looks like someone intentionally smeared the information."

"Markie, can you go back and get an image of the other buoy? Maybe it is just this one that got smeared," requested Greg.

"Yes, I can do that," responded Markie.

Markie jumped back in the water, swam over to the other buoy, took an image of it, and returned to the boat. The boys looked at Markie's screen on his chest plate. They moved the image of the buoy around on the screen. After studying it, they agreed the lettering on the second buoy was definitely written by the same person. In addition, the lettering was smeared even more than the first one they read.

"Whoa, why would someone from Seattle come here to do crabbing?" asked Greg.

"Beats me. There are a lot of crabbing areas between here and Seattle," said Topher.

Rick thought and added, "Maybe someone is here visiting a friend and randomly put their pot over here."

"Yeah, you are probably right," said Topher.

Greg shook his head in agreement and said, "Well, should we drop our pot here too?"

"No, let's set our heading at 330 degrees and go out about 200 feet away from these buoy markers," Topher suggested.

The boys agreed and off they went to hopefully find a new prime spot.

After all of the pots were dropped into the water, the boys set a course back to their dock. It had been a busy day and they were beginning to get tired and hungry. Their minds were busy thinking about the events of the day. It seemed like it should be late at night. They had seen their families off and discovered an alien robot in their dormitory. They learned about Markie and his galaxy and now they had a mystery crabber invading their prime crabbing spot. They were mentally and physically exhausted. When they had cleared the cove a man in a boat had started to enter the cove, but when he saw them he turned around and headed back out of the cove. Then, he just stopped and appeared to be waiting until they left.

In a short time, the boys arrived at their dock and went up to the cabin. They decided to relax and watch their favorite television show.

Greg said, "Markie, we are going to watch a television show, you might find it interesting."

Markie sat down next to Greg. Aaron curled up on the sofa next to Rick and laid his head on Rick's lap. Within a short time, the boys and Aaron were fast asleep.

Markie watched the television until the boys fell asleep and then he decided to start researching the habits of boys and people from Earth. If you were to look at Markie, you would have thought he was sleeping too.

After an hour of accessing information in his Internal Knowledge Unit, Markie walked into the kitchen. Aaron heard him moving around and followed him into the kitchen. Aaron was hungry, so he started pawing at the kitchen cupboard door. Markie opened up the door and saw a box with a dog on it. He saw Aaron's dog bowl and after reading the instructions, gave Aaron a serving of his dog food. Aaron looked at Markie with a new sense of appreciation.

Markie then began to access information on how to feed the boys. Markie had watched Rick's mom in the kitchen when she was there. His mom did not see Markie because he stayed under the table and out of sight.

The boys woke up to the smell of something wonderful coming from the kitchen. They tumbled into the kitchen thinking it must be Rick's mom cooking. Instead, they found Markie standing by the table that had been set for dinner. There was hot food in the oven.

To Markie, Topher said as he pointed to the table and oven, "Did you do this?"

Markie replied, "I accessed my IKU and was able to learn you need to eat three meals each day. I looked into the refrigerator and the kitchen cupboards. I used my scanner to make an inventory of the staples you have. Next, I ran the list of staples into my recipe search mode and found a recipe for Chicken Pot Pie. Therefore, I made a Chicken Pot Pie for your third meal of the day."

Markie had even made a small one for Aaron.

"This is FANTASTIC!" they shouted.

The boys sat down to eat and Aaron was prancing around his bowl waiting for his pot pie.

"Markie how did you make this pie with your paws?"

asked Topher.

Markie held up his front paws and extended them out. When he extended them the pads of his paws became like fingers. He showed them how he could use his pads just like the boys could use their fingers. He told them his pads were not sensitive to heat or cold.

"Markie, aren't you going to eat," said Greg.

"No, I don't eat. My fuel source is obtained by the water and the sun. I am full," he said.

Through mouths full of the pot pie, they told Markie that it was the best pot pie they had ever eaten. Markie was glad that he had helped the boys again. They went over and gave Markie a rub behind the ears. Markie knew this was a sign of affection because he saw the boys do it to Aaron and he could tell that Aaron really liked it. At this moment, Markie was feeling happier than he had felt in a long time.

After the boys cleaned up the dishes, they went down to the docks. They were going out on the water to check on their crab pots. They wanted to check on them before it got too late.

Topher was steering the boat as Greg read off the coordinates. Rick had the CRC card with him to record their catch. The first few pots were very successful and they were happy with their catch. The next pot was hard to bring up; there was a lot of seaweed that had gotten wrapped around it. At first they thought they had a huge catch, but when they saw the massive amount of seaweed they became disappointed. Rick almost fell in the water trying to lift it out of the water.

Topher said, "I have an idea -- let's use the pole to

knock the seaweed off the crab pot."

"Good thinking," said Greg.

Topher grabbed the pole and started lifting the seaweed off the pot. However, when he was poking the seaweed, he knocked the buoy line off the crab pot and it fell into the water. The crab pot sank faster than the boys could retrieve it. Quickly, Markie jumped into the water and dove down after the pot.

Rick cautioned him, "Markie be careful!"

It seemed like a very long time had passed. The boys were standing anxiously peering into the water. Aaron was hanging his head down trying to get a scent.

The boys heard a familiar sound coming from the other side of the boat, then a splash, a clink, followed by a thud. They turned around and there was Markie. He had retrieved the crab pot and threw it in the boat. There were four crabs inside the pot.

"Oh, thank goodness you are OK," they said to Markie.

"You have to be careful, Markie, we don't want you to get hurt," said Greg while Rick and Topher nodded in agreement.

"Thank you," said Markie.

He was coming to realize the boys cared for him and that he liked them too.

"I didn't notice any crabs in the pot earlier," commented Rick.

The boys thanked Markie again for saving the crab pot and Aaron gave him a lick.

"We need to get the crabs to Doe Bay, but I don't think Markie should go with us. I don't want anyone to see him," said Greg.

"Yes, that is a good idea," said Rick and to Markie he said, "Markie, we want you to stay in the cabin when we go to Doe Bay. We should only be gone about two hours or less."

Markie replied, "OK, I can swim to the docks from here and then meet you at the cabin in a couple of hours. I want to look in an area not too far from here for my transporter."

Then without saying any more, he jumped into the water and was gone. Aaron looked out over the side of the boat for Markie.

The boys were quiet for a while. Normally, they would be chatting away about their catch. They had enjoyed their time with Markie and suddenly realized that when he found his transporter he would leave.

Aaron's barking broke their silence. They had rounded the outcrop and were approaching the Doe Bay Café's dock. Mr. Hamilton was down at the dock talking with one of the fisherman when the boys approached.

"Hey there mates, it looks like you have a good amount of crabs for me," declared Mr. Hamilton.

Proudly they answered him, "Yes sir, Mr. Hamilton. We sure do."

They handed the cooler to Mr. Hamilton and he whistled and said, "You sure do!"

Aaron with his tail wagging was on his way to see Mrs. Hamilton. Aaron could eat every hour of the day.

"You boys are here a little late today. I didn't think you were going crabbing today since your folks just left," said Mrs. Hamilton as she opened up the side door. "Did you boys want some crab cakes? It won't take me long to fry up a fresh batch."

"No, we are good. We had dinner already, but thank you," replied Rick.

Mr. Hamilton went into his office and came out with their pay.

"Wow, thank you very much sir," they all said at once.

"You boys look tired," said Mr. Hamilton. "You need to take a day off and relax. You caught enough for two days. Are you going over to see Mrs. Sweet?"

"No sir," said Greg "We are going to head back to the cabin. We have some chores to do."

When the boys left, Mr. Hamilton said to Mrs. Hamilton, "Myrtle, the boys are working very hard."

Within a short time, the boys were arriving at their dock. They didn't see any signs of Markie and became worried. They docked the boat in record time and headed up to the cabin.

There in the middle of the sofa was Markie and he appeared to be fast asleep. Topher walked over to him and patted his head and rubbed his ear. Aaron gave him a big lick and nudged him.

Markie's eyes opened up and he was happy to see the boys.

"Did you find your transporter?" asked Rick.

"No, but one day I will," he said.

Remembering about the Morse code signals, Greg asked, "Markie, do you think you could teach us how to do Morse code signals? I think that it would be fun to learn."

Rick and Topher agreed and Markie said he would teach them how to send Morse code signals.

"Then, maybe if we meet another robot alien we won't send a garbled message," said Rick.

Through yawns Topher added, "But, first we should get ready for bed. I don't know about you guys, but I am really tired. It seems like this has been a very long day."

The boys went up to the dormitory, got on their pj's, and fell into their beds. Within seconds they were asleep. Markie and Aaron curled up together on one of the spare beds.

Chapter 6

Rick was the first one to awaken. He yawned, rubbed his eyes, and quietly got out of bed. Topher and Greg were sound asleep. During the night, Aaron had crawled into bed with Rick. When Rick got out of bed, Aaron got up and followed him downstairs.

Rick walked over to the cupboard to get a glass, but then remembered the large paper cups in the other cupboard. His mom had brought them over from the mainland on her last visit. He decided to use a paper cup, so he wouldn't have to wash a cup when he was done. He poured himself a glass of milk and went over to the couch. He sat down and drank his milk. Aaron jumped up on the couch next to him.

Suddenly, Rick remembered Markie.

"Aaron, where is Markie?" asked Rick.

Aaron looked up at Rick and tilted his head as if he were trying to understand what Rick was asking.

"Hmm, I didn't see him in the dormitory this morning," he quietly said to Aaron.

Rick got up and started looking around the lower level bedrooms, but Markie was nowhere to be seen.

"Did I dream we had an alien robot dog?" he said to Aaron.

Aaron walked over to the door and pawed it.

"OK boy, I'll let you out," said Rick. "Oh yuck, it's raining," he said as he opened the door.

Rick stood under the cover of the porch and watched as Aaron trotted off to make his morning rounds. He kept looking for signs of Markie, but couldn't see any. He looked back at the front door and realized he had to unlock the door to let Aaron out. Therefore, Markie couldn't have left by the front door.

Aaron came back quickly. He wasn't interested in staying outside any longer than he needed to this morning. Rick dried his paws like his mother had instructed him to do and let him back into the cabin.

Rick walked over to the back door and checked it. It was still locked too. Rick walked back upstairs and looked all around the dormitory. Markie was nowhere to be found.

Rick went back downstairs and kept trying to decide if Markie was a dream. Then he asked himself if he took any pictures of Markie. No, he didn't.

He thought, what do I have to prove Markie exists? He remembered he had searched his computer for the

Markarian Galaxy. He went over to his computer and looked at his search history, but it did not show him searching for the Markarian Galaxy.

Soon, Greg and Topher were slowly walking downstairs.

Upon seeing them, Rick asked, "Hey guys, did we meet an alien robot dog yesterday?"

Greg laughingly said, "No, why?"

Topher added with a laugh, "Rick, did you get hit on the head last night?"

Rick's mouth fell open and then Topher said, "We got you! Where is Markie?"

"Ah man, don't mess with me. I was beginning to think I was dreaming it all. He isn't here."

"He probably went to look for his Intergalactic Transporter," said Greg.

Rick added, "I kept thinking I had no proof that he exists. I didn't take a photo of him."

"Remember Rick, your mom saw him," confirmed Topher.

"Yeah, well maybe we can get a picture of him with our cell phones," said Rick.

Topher walked over and looked outside and then said, "It doesn't look like we will be crabbing today. It is raining and the seas look rough."

The boys heard a clunking sound coming from the front porch. They ran over to see if it was Markie.

Topher opened up the door and there was Markie. He said, "Markie, we are glad to see you! Come on in."

Greg said to Markie, "Rick was afraid that he was dreaming you existed when he didn't see you this morning."

Then, Rick made a request of Markie, "Would you leave us a note when you go out, so we will know where you are?"

After Rick said that he finally understood why his mom always asked him to leave her notes. He thought to himself he would never forget to text her or leave her a note.

"Yes, I will," said Markie. "Will you go crabbing today?"

Greg answered, "No, the seas are too rough and it is raining."

"I have an idea," said Topher. "After breakfast, maybe Markie will teach us Morse code?"

"That would be great," said Rick and Greg as they looked at Markie.

"I would be happy to teach you the Morse code signals," responded Markie.

Rick walked over and got his cereal out of the cupboard. He looked at his large paper cup and thought it would be perfect to put his cereal in. He poured his cereal in the large paper cup and then poured his milk over the cereal. He grabbed a spoon and thought this will work great.

Upon seeing what Rick had done, Greg said, "Hey Topher, look at what Rick did. Great idea, I like minimal clean-up."

The boys used the paper cups for their cereal, too.

Topher added, "All we will have to do is to wash the spoon! But, what about all the paper waste?"

Quickly, Rick responded, "We can save the cups and

stack them inside each other. Then, when we build our bonfire, we can put them in the center and use them as tender to start the fire."

"Good thinking," they both answered.

Aaron was standing by his bowl barking and Greg said, "OK, I'll get it, but no paper cups for you. You might eat the dog food and paper cup."

After the boys were finished with their breakfast, Markie told them to get paper and pencils to write down the Morse code signals.

Once the boys were gathered in the family room, Markie began to explain how Morse code works.

He explained there are several different versions of Morse code. The original is the American version. The Continental or Gerke was used on German railways. The current Morse code used is the International Morse Code and told them, because of this, they will learn the International Morse code.

Markie continued to say Morse code is a system of dots and dashes that can be heard or visualized using lights.

"Oh, so when I was waving my flashlight around and turning it off and on, you thought they were the dots and dashes," said Rick.

"Yes," answered Markie. "Look at my screen. Write down the alphabet letter and the corresponding dots and dashes. When you are done, I will tell you more about how to use it."

The boys were busy writing down the Morse code.

Greg said, "Markie, why don't you read off the dots and dashes for us as we write them down."

" replied Markie.

...ead the following:

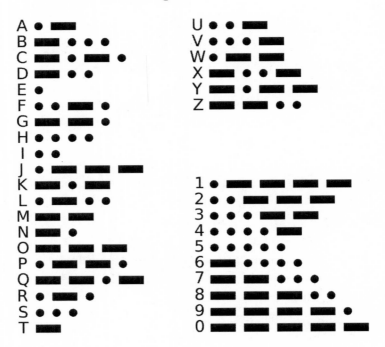

The boys were busy writing down the Morse code as Markie dictated the dots and dashes. He told them the dots are read as dit and the dashes are read as dah.

Markie than demonstrated with a tap on the table what a dot sounded like followed by a dash. Next, he had the boys practice the letters.

"This is cool," said Topher.

Markie told them the users of Morse code have simplified the words, just as the boys do when they are texting each other. So instead of writing the word *are,* they would code only the letter *r.*

"You mean we aren't the first generation to think of abbreviating words?" asked Rick with surprise.

"No," answered Markie and then continued, "your great-grandfathers used abbreviated words when sending Morse code signals during World War II."

"Wowww," they all said in unison.

"Let's each tap out one letter of the alphabet and see if the others can understand what that letter is," suggested Greg.

"OK, here it goes," said Rick and he tapped out *dit dah dit*.

"*R*,"said Topher.

Topher than tapped out *dah*.

"*T*," said Greg and then said, "I am going to tap out a word with two letters."

Markie said, "Remember, in-between each alphabetical letter there is a pause of three counts and between each word is a pause of seven counts."

Greg tapped out *dit dit dit dit   dit dit*.

Rick and Topher yelled together, "Hi."

The boys continued to practice sending Morse code words to each other throughout the afternoon. They were having a lot of fun memorizing the alphabet in Morse code.

Rick said to Markie, "I will write down a list of words we abbreviate when we send text messages, so you will know them too."

"Thank you, Rick," replied Markie.

By evening, the rain finally stopped and it was beginning to clear

Greg looked outside and said, "It looks like it will

start clearing this evening and through the weekend. Our families will be able to come out to the island tomorrow."

The boys were looking forward to seeing their families and wanted to ask them if they knew a man named John Graham.

Mr. & Mrs. Ebert and Mary were the first to arrive in the morning. As always, there were many supplies to unload from their boat. Greg was helping them unload when Markie started walking out of Rick's cabin. Unfortunately, he didn't see Markie coming out of the cabin, but Mary did.

Mary shouted out to her parents, "Check out the robot dog."

Greg spun his head around and almost fainted. Quickly, he recuperated from his shock and said, "Oh, look what Rick sent to the docks to greet you. He was supposed to wait until this evening and we were going to do a grand unveiling of our latest project."

Mary wasn't paying attention to what Greg was saying and ran up to Markie and asked, "What did you guys name him? He is so-o-o cute!"

"We named him Markie," Greg answered.

Greg's parents were busy unloading the supplies and didn't pay much attention to Markie.

Greg walked over and pretended to turn Markie off and say, "I'll take him back to Rick's cabin and I will be right back."

Off he ran with Markie in tow and Markie quietly said, "Your sister, Mary, is nice." Markie then turned his head to look at Mary.

"You need to stay inside until this evening," ordered Greg.

Rick was leaving the cabin to go to the docks. He heard on the marine radio his parents and sister would soon be arriving. Markie nodded his head to Greg. Then Markie went upstairs to look out the window at the boys' families arriving on the island. He was eager to get to know them.

Everyone was busy getting settled in and Markie stayed upstairs in the dormitory. Rick's sister, Regina, took her backpack upstairs and proceeded to set out all of her princess paraphernalia. Rick was busy and forgot about Markie being upstairs in the dormitory when his sister went upstairs.

Suddenly, he heard some giggling, laughter, and the sound of Aaron jumping off and on the beds upstairs. His mom heard the noise too and said, "Rick will you go and check on your sister while I get dinner started?"

He ran upstairs and when he looked into the dormitory, he saw Regina sitting on the floor with Aaron and Markie sitting in front of her. She had a princess crown on Aaron, Markie, and herself. She had put princess stickers on Aaron's fur and on Markie's body, which probably explained why Aaron was jumping around – trying to escape no doubt. Regina was in the process of putting lipstick on Markie when Rick walked in.

"Whoa, what are you doing, Regina?" said Rick. "You can't put that stuff on the dogs."

"Yes, I can," she said rather curtly. "I asked Markie if she would like to be a princess and she said, 'Yes.' So

I am making her a princess."

Rick retorted, "First, Markie is a boy. Secondly, he is mine and I don't want you putting lipstick and crowns on him."

"Tish, tish, Markie, we will have to wait to play princess later," said Regina to Markie. She turned her head and gave Rick a snubbed look.

Rick was upset and went downstairs to tell his mom what Regina had done to his robot. His mom laughed and promised to talk to Regina about not making the dogs princesses.

That evening at the bonfire get-together, the families were all chatting and telling stories.

Topher said, "Hey Rick, why don't you get Markie and we can show him to our families."

Mary added, "He is soo cute. I saw him earlier today."

Regina chimed in, "Yes, he is nice and let's me play princess party."

Greg said, "What? Princess party?"

Rick replied, "Don't ask!"

Rick brought Markie to the bonfire and everyone looked at him. They thought the boys had done a great job of building and programming him. In the right light, Rick could still see remnants of lipstick and possibly rouge on Markie's face.

Greg leaned over and said to Markie, "I like that color of rouge and lipstick on you."

Rick made a grumbling sound.

Markie turned his head and said, "Thank you. Regina said it is Princess Pink."

The boys laughed and rolled their eyes. Markie turned, looked at Regina, and winked at her. When she saw him wink at her, she smiled, and winked back.

Aaron was busy trying to get some of the stickers off his fur. Then, he started to lick his toes.

Topher looked at Aaron's paws and said, "Looks like Aaron didn't escape the princess party either. He has pink toe nail polish on."

Rick looked at his sister and said, "Regina!"

She smiled and Aaron went over to Rick and gave him a lick.

"Yeah, I know boy. I'll keep a closer eye on Regina and her princess make-up."

Topher said to the parents, "Does anyone know a John Graham from Seattle?"

After giving it some thought, the parents shook their heads no.

Topher's mom, Susan said, "Why?"

He responded, "We saw his buoy markers out on the bay and didn't recognize the name. We wondered if it was someone new who had moved into the area."

"No," they responded.

Rick's dad asked, "What is the boat's registration number? You can find out who it is by their number."

Then he added, "Are there any problems?"

"No," said Rick. "We know most of the fishermen and didn't recognize his name. He comes very early to drop off his pots and then comes back later in a different boat to pick them up late at night."

"Well, you boys know you can't lay your pots out before sunrise and you aren't supposed to be out on the water after sunset," stated Greg's dad.

They answered, "Yes," and the dads looked at each other with concern.

Rick Sr. said to the boys, "If you see anything strange you need to let us and Captain MacArthur know."

"Yes sir," they answered.

That night when Rick and Regina went to the dormitory to sleep, Regina said, "Rick, Markie wants to sleep with me tonight. Can he?"

When Regina's head was turned, Rick looked at Markie and he shook his head *yes*.

Rick replied to Regina, "Sure, but no princess party make-up on him."

Regina smiled from ear to ear and she, Markie, and Aaron jumped into her bed. She had an arm around each of them.

At some point during the night, Rick woke up and looked over at his sister. She, Aaron, and Markie looked very peaceful. Markie opened up his eyes and blinked the following message to Rick, *dit dit dit dit   dit dit.* Rick tapped back the same message to Markie.

Just as quickly as the weekend arrived, it was over. The boys enjoyed spending time with their families. The boys were happy to share their great crabbing successes with them.

After the families set sail to Bellingham Bay, the boys gathered to discuss their plans for the week.

"Rick's dad had a good idea," said Topher. "We should write down the registration numbers from the boats. Then, we can find out who the owners are."

"Yeah," said Rick. "We can watch out for them.

Topher, bring your binoculars and we can use them. I don't want to send Markie out into the water. They might see him."

"OK, I'll go get them from my cabin," said Topher.

Greg asked, "Captain MacArthur will know how to look up the registration numbers, but what are we going to tell him so he will look them up? We don't want him to get suspicious."

Rick said, "We will need to think of a good reason."

"Well, first we need to get the numbers and then we can work on getting the information. I think it is going to be hard enough to get the numbers from the boats," said Topher.

The boys agreed that getting the boat registration numbers from the sides of the boats was going to be difficult.

It was getting late and Aaron started scratching at the front door.

"OK, you want to make one last trip outside for the night," said Greg as he opened up the front door.

Markie and Aaron both went outside. Then, just before Greg shut the door, he heard a boat engine out on the water. By the sound of the engine, it was coming towards their cove.

Chapter 7

When Greg first heard the sound of the boat engine, he thought for an instant it might be one of their parents returning to their docks. It was late and the only light was coming from the glow of the full moon on the water. He strained to see who was coming. He turned the porch light off, so he could see out on the water more clearly. The glare of the porch light was making it hard for him to see. Suddenly, the boat rounded the corner and he could tell by the outline of the boat it was neither of their parents' boats. Instead, it appeared to be their mystery crabber.

Greg whispered, "Aaron, Markie come here." He reasoned Aaron must have heard the engine noise and wanted to go outside to investigate it.

Aaron and Markie did not return, so he said softly, but more commandingly, "Aaron, hamburger." Aaron and Markie's heads went up and they trotted over to Greg. He called Aaron over to him because he didn't want Aaron to start barking and scare the mystery crabber away. Bending low by the doorway, he called out to Rick and Topher, "Guys hurry up! Turn off the inside lights and come here."

Quickly, Rick turned off the cabin lights and the boys slipped out of the house. They saw Greg crouching low behind the bushes. Aaron and Markie were beside him. Aaron thought he was playing a game with Greg and Markie looked around. Markie was trying to understand what was bothering Greg about the man in the boat.

"What's going on?" asked Topher.

Rick looked out over the water and said, "Who's that?"

Greg softly answered, "I don't know, but it looks like our mystery crabber. He just showed up."

They were peering out on the water. By now, the man was slowing his engine down as he coasted into their cove. They saw him drop two crab pots down, look around, start up his engine, and take off.

"Could you see the registration number on his boat?" asked Rick.

"No," said Greg it was too dark. I hope he didn't see us. I had turned the porch light off before he rounded the corner.

"Something is definitely not right," said Topher. "No one drops off crab pots this late."

Markie asked, "What are you afraid of Greg?"

"I don't know, I just know that something isn't right about this mystery crabber," answered Greg.

The boys went back inside and decided to keep the lights off inside. They locked the doors and gathered upstairs. Rick lowered the blinds and closed the slats. They turned the closet light on, so the room would be dimly lit.

"We should keep watch over the cove tonight and see if he returns," said Rick.

"We could take turns staying up and watching out the window," stated Topher.

Greg said, "I'll take the first watch. I am wide-awake."

"OK," said Rick and Topher. "Wake us up, if you see anything."

Greg nodded his head and pulled a chair up to the window. Aaron climbed in bed with Rick and Markie sat next to Greg.

After an hour of sitting and watching, Greg fell asleep. He awoke when he felt something pulling at him. It was Markie.

Markie said, "Greg wake up. He's back."

Then, Markie went over to Rick and Topher and woke them up. They went over to the window and peeked out through the slits of the blind.

"I'll get my binoculars and see if I can see the numbers on the boat," said Topher.

Rick said, "I can only see the outline of the boat and it looks different. This one has a different placement of the cockpit. It appears to be farther back and the other one was near the bow."

"It looks like only one person in the boat," said Greg.

Topher added, "He is pulling up the crab pots. Now, he is taking something out. Can anyone see what he is taking out?"

"No, but the way he is handling the catch, it can't be crabs," said Greg.

"Did you see that? Whatever it was, it briefly glowed when the moonlight shined on it," commented Rick.

Topher, with a surprised tone, added, "He reached down, took something else out from his boat, and put it into the crab pot."

"What in the world is going on?" they asked.

Greg continued, "One man comes, puts something in the crab pot. A second guy arrives, takes something out that glowed briefly, and then put something inside the crab pot. This is definitely strange."

They almost thought the mystery crabber heard them, because suddenly he jerked up, looked around, and wiped his nose on his sleeve. The boys got very quiet. Then he quickly threw the crab pots overboard and started up his engine. Off he went into the night.

"What was that about?" asked Rick.

"Boy, I don't know. Do you think the first crabber will be back tonight?" asked Topher.

They looked at each other and shook their heads yes. By this time, the boys were wide-awake with the mysterious happenings in their cove.

Greg broke the silence and said, "Let's stay up and see if the other guy comes back tonight."

Both Rick and Topher agreed to stay up and keep

a watch out for the first crabber, because now they believed there are two mystery crabbers.

After an hour of trying to stay awake, the boys began to doze off. Markie continued to sit and watch for the first mystery crabber to return.

It was almost sunrise when Markie headed out the door of the cabin. He looked over in the cove and the buoys were still there. He left the boys the following note:

Rick, Topher, Greg, and Aaron,
I have gone to the cliff area to search for some of my parts. I left them there for safekeeping. I will be back before sunrise.
Markie

Markie was careful to go up the cliff area along the wooded side, so no one would see him. He was happy to find the spot where he had left the parts to his cloaking unit. He was in the process of reconnecting some of the cloaking unit parts and storing the damaged parts in his storage compartment when he heard the sound of a boat engine. He walked over to the cliff area and saw their mystery crabber heading into their cove. As soon as the mystery crabber reached the buoys, he started pulling up the crab pots. Markie hid very carefully behind a large Madrona tree; however, he wanted to get a closer look at the mystery crabber. Therefore, he stepped near a smaller bush to get a closer look and as he did his foot stepped on a dry twig. It made a loud cracking sound. The mystery crabber quickly looked up and Markie crouched low. Markie stood very still, so he wouldn't make any noise. The crabber looked around the cliff area for a while and then went back to his task at hand. Markie used his telescopic vision to see what he was taking out of the crab pot. It was a black plastic bag.

The mystery crabber looked inside the plastic bag and moved the contents around as if he were examining them very closely. Then, he quickly looked around and dropped the empty crab pots with attached buoys back in the water. He started up his engine and slowly and quietly set a course out of the small cove. Markie remembered the boys were trying to get the numbers on the boat. He positioned himself, so he could see the registration numbers on the side of the boat. As the small boat changed direction and headed southwest, Markie got a good view of the numbers. He used his camera and captured an image of it and the side view of the mystery crabber.

When the mystery crabber changed course, Markie went to the other side of the cliff to watch where he was going. He was headed towards the west coast of Cypress Island. When the boat rounded Cypress Island, Markie lost sight of him.

Markie knew this was significant information he needed to share with the boys. After gathering up the remaining parts for his cloaking unit, he returned to the cabin.

As Markie approached the cabin, he could tell the boys were already up as Aaron was on his way outside to make his morning rounds. For a short time, Markie forgot what he was going to do and followed Aaron around. He was mimicking Aaron's morning ritual. As they were making their rounds, Aaron's head suddenly went up and he started looking around. Markie put his head up too and within a short time, the sound of a boat engine could be heard. By the sound of the engine, it was approaching their cove. Markie hid behind Aaron. Instinctively, Aaron turned and gave Markie a lick as if to assure him that it will be OK. Markie then saw it was the second mystery crabber.

Since the boys always left their marine radio on, Markie sent them the following message using his on-board communication unit:

Dah dah   dah dit dah dit,   dit dit dit dit   dit
dit dah dit   dit (M C here)

M C is shortened for mystery crabber. The boys heard the message and Topher grabbed his binoculars. The boys slipped out of the house and crouched low behind the bushes. Markie kept Aaron off to the side, so he wouldn't start barking.

Topher was reading off the numbers on the boat and Rick was writing it down in the dirt. Topher got the first five letters of RI 081 before the first mystery crabber pulled the empty crab pots out of the water, secured the pots in his boat, and left the cove. As he left the cove, his heading was southeast.

As soon as he was gone, Markie and Aaron went over to the boys.

"Good job, Markie," said Greg with excitement.

"Aaron was the first to hear the engine sound and I hid behind him, so the mystery crabber wouldn't see me," answered Markie. "I couldn't see him clearly without exposing myself. Therefore, I sent you the Morse code message."

"We make a great team!" said Rick.

Markie then shared with the boys how the second mystery crabber arrived in the cove just before sunrise. He told them the second crabber pulled the crab pots out of the water and then pulled a black plastic bag out of the crab pots. After he emptied the crab pots, he lowered them into the water.

"Are you sure it was a black plastic bag?" asked Greg.

"Yes," answered Markie and then continued "I took an image of the side of the boat with the boat numbers. I was careful and he didn't see me. When he left, his heading was southwest. He steered his boat towards the west coast of Cypress Island before I lost sight of him."

"I don't understand why he would lower empty crab pots into the water," thought Topher out loud.

The boys gathered around Markie's screen as he showed them the image.

Rick asked, "Can we zoom in on the image?"

"Yes," confirmed Markie. "If you want to zoom in on the image, tap twice on the area you want to enlarge. If you want to lighten the image draw a line across the image."

"Oh, this is great!" they said.

Rick ran and got their notebook and asked them to read off the boat registration numbers. Topher read off the numbers RH 0521 TE as Rick wrote them down.

Greg added, "Now, we have one of the boat numbers and a partial number on the second boat. All we have to do is to get the names and addresses of the owners."

"No small task," moaned Rick.

Topher was still looking at the image on Markie's chest plate and said, "Guys, look at the mystery crabber. I zoomed in on him and lightened the image. I think it is a guy, but it is hard to tell for certain. He is wearing a black hoodie and it's pulled up over his head. He is wearing jeans."

"Are there any insignias on the hoodie? You know, like a team sport," asked Rick.

"No," replied Topher. "He has short white hair."

"Yes," agreed the boys as they looked at the screen.

"Guys, remember in math class when we learned to do ratios? We could figure out his approximate height by using ratios. All we have to do is measure the boat on Markie's screen and we can calculate his height. The boat is a 16-footer based on the model number on the side of the boat," calculated Rick.

"Great thinking," said Greg.

Looking at Markie's screen and using a ruler they measured the length of the boat. It measured four inches on the screen.

"OK, so if it measures four inches then one-fourth of an inch represents one foot," reasoned Topher.

Rick took the ruler and measured the height of the guy in the boat from the top side of the boat to the top of his head. Rick measured one inch.

Greg calculated, "If he measures one inch then he stands approximately four feet tall above the side of the boat. Plus, the inside boat depth is about two feet. Therefore, our mystery crabber is about six feet tall."

"Yeah, that is right," agreed Rick and Topher.

Topher added, "We need to gather intel (intelligence information) on the mystery crabbers and make a chart."

"Great idea," said Rick. "Also, we should make a map of where and approximately when our mystery crabbers have dropped and picked up crab pots in the area."

Greg said with conviction, "Yes and then maybe we will be able to see a pattern and predict where they might appear next."

The boys were excited as they were beginning to make a plan to find out what was going on with their mystery crabbers, as they were calling them.

Markie was looking at the boys and tried to understand why they were interested in the mystery crabber.

Seeing the puzzled look on Markie's face Rick said, "Markie, Captain MacArthur told us there were troublemakers in the area and we think these guys might be the ones. However, we can't go to Captain MacArthur with the little information we have. We want to gather additional information to share with him."

Markie asked, "What is a troublemaker?"

Greg answered, "A troublemaker is someone who does something wrong."

Markie continued, "Can they hurt you?"

"Yes, that is why we have to be careful," added Rick.

"I'll get a large piece of paper and make a map of the area, then we can mark down their known crab pot drops with the dates and approximate times," stated Rick.

Rick ran upstairs to the dormitory where they had all kinds of paper and supplies.

Greg said, "I'll start writing down the information we know about each crabber and their boats."

Greg made a chart with the following information:

Mystery Crabber # 1 (MC1) male, black hoodie, white short hair, approximately six feet tall, 16-foot boat with registration numbers RH0521TE, puts something in the crab pot that glows in the moonlight, returns to remove black plastic bag, doesn't put anything in the crab pot, but lowers it into the water. Is he John Graham or does he know him?

Mystery Crabber # 2 (MC2) boat with registration numbers RI081???, removes what MC1 puts into the crab pot, puts a black plastic bag in the crab pot, lowers it into the water, returns when the crab pot is empty, and takes the empty crab pots with him or her. Is he John Graham or does he know him?

He read it to Topher and Rick and said, "Did I get all the facts right? Do, I need to add anything?"

Markie said, "Yes, there is one more clue."

"What's that?" they asked.

"Based on my knowledge search on how boys and girls act, MC2 must be a male. He wiped his nose on his sleeve. Also, he primarily used his left hand. Therefore, he is left-handed," stated Markie.

"That's a funny observation, but I think you are on to something," said Greg.

They agreed to add the facts that MC2 was probably a male and left-handed.

"How is the map coming, Rick?" asked Topher.

"I am almost done and ready for us to list the dates and times the mystery crabbers have been going to the various places on the map," stated Rick.

Rick finished drawing the map and showed the boys.

"Neat map, Rick," the boys said.

"Thanks. I put Cypress, Obstruction, Blakely, Sinclair, and of course Orcas Islands on the map," confirmed Rick.

"OK, let's see if we can piece together the dates and places of the drops and pick-ups for each of our mystery crabbers," said Greg.

"Our first clue is the mystery crabber put his crab pots in Lost Cove some time before Sunday afternoon," stated Greg.

Rick drew a boat with a MC on it and wrote Sunday before 1:00 pm and then said, "But, we don't know when he came back because the buoys were gone when we returned in the evening."

Markie added, "Do you remember a boat that was arriving in Lost Cove when we were leaving?"

"Yes," said Topher "I forgot about that. He seemed to be waiting outside the cove and then went back into the cove when we left."

"You're right, I was very tired and didn't pay attention to him," replied Greg.

Rick, wrote down on the map mystery crabber returns at 1:00 pm and said, "Presumably he removed the pots because we didn't see them when we returned that evening."

Markie said, "When you guys went to Doe Bay Café to sell the crabs to Mr. Hamilton, I went to look for my transporter. I saw MC1 lowering two crab pots into the water near Obstruction Pass. Then, when I went back out to look for my transporter the next morning, I saw MC2 removing something from the crab pots and put something back into them before lowering the crab pots back into the water."

"So, Sunday evening MC1 puts two crab pots in the water. Monday before sunrise MC2 removes something and puts something else back into the crab pots," stated Topher.

Rick drew a boat on the map at Obstruction Pass and wrote down the dates and times.

Greg said, "Our next encounter with the mystery crabbers was last night and this morning in our cove."

Rick added this information onto the map.

The boys, Markie, and Aaron sat and looked at their map and Greg's chart on the mystery crabbers.

Aaron walked over and brought a rolled-up marine navigational chart for crabbing season, dropped it by the boys, and barked.

"Hey look, Aaron is trying to help," they laughed.

"Wait a minute, he is helping," said Rick. "The mystery crabbers have been putting their crab pots near other crab pots, which mean they have only been putting them in designated crabbing areas."

"Yes, but why would they put their crab pots in our cove?" asked Greg. "It is a designated crabbing area, but there were no other crab pots in the cove."

"I don't know, it doesn't make sense, but I think we should narrow our search down to crabbing areas," asserted Rick.

They agreed to search for the mystery crabbers in designated grabbing areas. They hung the marine navigational chart next to the map Rick had drawn. Aaron sniffed it and then barked. The boys laughed, patted Aaron on the head, and then Rick rubbed his ears.

"I wish we had noticed the mystery crabbers sooner because we would know if they have been returning to certain areas," said Topher. "Now, how are we going to get the information on the owners of the boats?"

Greg replied, "When we take our catch into Mr. Hamilton this afternoon, we can stop in at Captain MacArthur's office. We can talk to him about boat registration numbers."

"Good plan," they answered.

As they were getting into the boat Rick turned and asked Markie, "What parts were you looking for in the woods?"

"My cloaking unit parts," replied Markie.

The boys stopped from loading up the gear and looked at Markie. They were not expecting him to say that.

Rick recovered from what Markie had said and

asked, "Your what? Did you find the parts to your cloaking unit?"

"Yes, I was looking for parts to my cloaking unit. However, I didn't find all of the parts, but at least I have enough of them to get started in repairing my cloaking unit," responded Markie. "I have an idea of where the missing pieces might be located. I will continue to look for those pieces in the next few days."

"Wow, is a cloaking unit what I think it is?" asked Greg.

Markie smiled and said, "Yes! It makes me appear invisible."

Chapter 8

"Let's set a course for Lost Cove," said Rick to Topher who was steering the boat. "Maybe we will see our mystery crabber there. And, if we don't, we might be able to catch some crabs."

Topher steered the boat towards Lost Cove and Greg asked Markie to tell them about his cloaking unit. Markie told them when he turns the cloaking unit on he becomes nearly invisible. If someone reached out and touched him they would feel him. Also, if he brushes up against something it would move. So, when he is in the cloaking mode he has to be careful not to disturb anything nearby.

"That is cool," said Rick.

Markie replied, "I had forgotten about it until we

were hiding from the mystery crabbers. If I had my cloaking unit working, I could have gone into the cloaking mode. Then, I could have taken an image of the second mystery crabber.

The boys were busy chatting about the cloaking unit as they began to near the entrance to Lost Cove. Aaron began pacing in the boat and then started to bark. Instinctively, Topher slowed down to see if there was something in the water. When he slowed the engine down, he heard the sound of another engine. It was coming from within Lost Cove.

"Maybe, it is our mystery crabber. Let's wait here and pretend to be moving our crab pots around in the boat," ordered Rick.

The boys started moving the crab pots around and looking at the buoys when the mystery crabber came out of the entrance to Lost Cove.

Topher said softly, "Let's try to look up at him without staring. We can pretend we are busy and barely notice him. I will look up briefly and wave at him."

"Markie, stay hidden," ordered Greg.

As the mystery crabber came out, Topher looked up and tried to get a good, but quick look at him. Then, Topher waved and yelled, "Hey."

When the mystery crabber saw him wave, he looked over at him, waved briefly, and then quickly turned around.

Under his breath and softly Topher said, "He is definitely MC1. He has white hair – like someone with very blonde hair. He doesn't appear to be very old. The numbers on the boat match up too."

"Look down Topher and I'll watch to see where he is going," said Greg. "He is headed southwest towards the west coast of Cypress Island. He is taking the same path as before."

Rick patted Aaron on the head and said, "Good job boy. If you had not barked we would have come upon him in the cove." To the boys and Markie he said, "We want to get close enough to see him, but not so close as to make him nervous."

"Should we drop our crab pots here in Lost Cove too?" asked Topher.

"Yes, but let's set them down in the south side of the cove," suggested Rick. "We don't want to get too close to their pots."

Greg said, "We should stay in the area and wait to see if MC2 shows up."

"Well, if my predictions are correct MC2 will be arriving from the southeast and leave the same way. We should take our boat outside of Lost Cove on the southeast side of the entrance. There is a little section of land that juts out and we can hide the boat behind the bushes. Then, when he leaves we can see what direction he is heading," proposed Greg.

"We should set up look-out points inside and on the cliff above Lost Cove. Markie can stay with one of us and get some images of the boat and mystery crabber," recommended Topher.

Rick added, "Also, one of us should be a look-out at the other side of the cove, just in case he decides to go in a different direction."

"Sounds like a good plan," they said.

"We will need to communicate with each other. So, whoever spots him first will need to signal the others. We can use our marine radios, set the channel to 42, and send Morse code signals. If MC2 is listening to his radio scanner, he won't know what we are saying," advised Topher.

"I'll take the boat and go outside the cove to the southeast side of the entrance. Aaron and I can sit behind the bushes near the shore. Then, if we see him come, we can let you know. While he is in the cove, we can get into the boat and get ready to follow him," said Rick.

"Markie and I can go above the cliff and wait for him there," said Greg.

Topher suggested that he would go to the cliff on the outside of the cove entrance on the southwest side. The boys wanted to make sure they covered all possible exit routes.

"Well, let's get our crab pots dropped and get ready," said Topher.

"It will probably be a while before MC2 arrives, so we can practice Morse code signaling in the meantime," proposed Rick.

Rick and Aaron took the boat and dropped Markie and Greg near the shoreline inside the cove. As they were getting out he said, "Once we are each in our positions, send the others a Morse code signal with your first initial and then IP for in position. And, don't forget, we will communicate on channel 42."

"Got it," said Greg and Topher.

Markie and Greg climbed the cliff and looked for a

good vantage point to see the crab pots and hopefully the mystery crabber.

Next, Rick dropped off Topher on the southwest side just outside the cove entrance. Topher, with his life jacket on, swam over to the shoreline and started to climb the steep cliff to get into position.

As Rick and Aaron were heading for the southeast side of the entrance to the cove, they received their first Morse code signal:

Dah dah dit, dit dit, dit dah dah dit (G IP)

Both Rick and Topher acknowledged Greg and Markie were in position. As soon as Rick and Aaron were on the southeast side of the entrance to the cove, Rick and Greg received the following message:

Dah, dit dit, dit dah dah dit (T IP)

OK, Topher was in position. Once the boat was secured to a low lying branch and hidden from sight, Rick sent the following message:

Dit dah dit, dit dit, dit dah dah dit (R IP)

The boys were sending each other messages and having fun, but then suddenly Aaron started to stir and Rick knew that meant someone was approaching. He quickly sent the following message:

Dah dah, dah dit dah dit dah dah dah dah dah, dit dit dit, dit (M COM SE)

Greg and Topher heard the message and understood MC2 was arriving from the southeast.

Rick and Aaron stayed hidden behind the bushes and watched MC2 approach Lost Cove. Rick couldn't see the boat registration numbers without exposing his hiding place. As soon as MC2 passed them, Rick and Aaron quietly got into their boat, loosened the line from the branch, and let the boat drift out towards the southeast. The plan was to start slowly heading southeast.

Greg sent the following message to the boys:

Dah dit dah dit,   dah dah, (C M)

Rick and Topher understood Greg and Markie could see the mystery crabber.

Greg and Markie were watching the crabber and, as luck would have it, they had a clear view of what he was doing. Markie recorded a lot of different images. He got the boat registration numbers, an image of MC2, and what he was putting in and taking out of the crab pots.

Greg sent a message to Topher and Rick:

Dah dit dah dit,   dit dah   dit dah dit dit (C AL)

Rick whispered to Aaron, "Great, Greg and Markie sent us a message they can see all that is going on with the mystery crabber."

Then, Greg sent the following message to Topher and Rick:

Dit dah dit dit,   dit dit dit,   dit (L SE)

Topher and Rick both knew it meant MC2 was leaving and headed southeast as they thought he might.

Rick and Aaron began heading southeast in anticipation that MC2 would choose the same heading.

In a short time, MC2 was moving quickly and was overcoming Rick. He passed Rick on his starboard side and as he passed Rick was able to get a good view of him and the boat registration number. Rick cranked up his engine a little, but not enough to look like he was trying to keep up with MC2. He was able to see MC2 change direction and head along the east coast of Sinclair Island.

Rick slowed his engine down and turned around and headed back to Lost Cove to pick up Greg, Markie, and Topher. He sent them the following message:

Dah dit dit dit   dit dah   dad dit dah,   dit dit dit dah dah dah   dah dah dah   da dit (BAK SOON)

The boys came down from the cliffs and waited for Rick in the cove.

As Rick was pulling into the cove, he could see Greg and Topher looking at Markie's screen. Rick steered the boat over to the buoys and checked the pots. They were full of crabs. He pulled them up and put them in the boat. He quickly sorted them, put the keepers in the cooler and threw only one of them back into the sea.

Topher yelled over to Rick, "It looks like we did great getting crabs and intel on our mystery crabber."

Rick gave them two thumbs up and then headed over to the shoreline. The boys waded out to the boat and jumped in.

Rick looked around and noticed the mystery crabber had also taken his crab pots up with him. Since there wasn't any danger of either of them returning, he said, "Let me see the images Markie was able to get."

Rick looked at the screen on Markie's chest plate and said, "Now we know the complete registration number for both boats and a description of the second mystery crabber. When we get back to the cabin, we can zoom in on what the mystery crabbers were putting in and taking out of the crab pots."

"MC2 is approximately 5 1/2 feet tall, medium build, dark hair, glasses, and a beard. The number on MC2's boat is RI0818SP," stated Topher.

"Let's go over to the Doe Bay Café and drop off the crabs, have dinner, and then go over and see Captain MacArthur," suggested Greg.

Whenever he heard the words Doe Bay Café, Aaron would always bark as if to say that idea has my vote. The boys turned and laughed.

"What about Markie?" asked Rick.

"He can walk up to the café and we'll tell everyone he is voice activated," advised Topher.

"Markie, you have to be quiet and not speak when we are there, but we will need your help when we are in the Captain's office. If we can get the Captain to bring the registration information on the boat owners up on his screen, you can take an image of it for us," said Rick.

The boys agreed it was a good plan and Markie was glad they were including him. Aaron was just happy to be going to the Doe Bay Café and to eat.

The boys were approaching the docks near Doe Bay Café and were both hungry and excited. Topher steered the boat close to the docks as Greg grabbed the line and jumped onto the dock. He secured the line to the dock cleat while Topher got out of the boat. Rick handed the cooler to Topher and Greg.

Before Rick got out of the boat, Topher asked him, "Do you have the notebook with the intel?"

Rick checked his back pocket and pulled out the notebook and said, "Yep, got it."

However, as he pulled out the notebook he snagged

his wallet and dropped it on the floor of the boat. When his wallet hit the floorboards, it opened up and the coins rolled out.

"Oh great!" he whined as the coins rolled around in the boat.

He scurried around picking up his coins when Greg offered to help him.

"No, I've got it," answered Rick.

Greg looked over and saw a coin part way under the spare life jacket and said, "Rick, there's one more near the spare life jacket."

Rick walked over and picked it up. He looked at it briefly and thought it looked different. He was distracted from looking at the unusual coin when he heard Aaron barking and running towards the Doe Bay Café. There was Markie happily running by his side.

"Oh geez, now we have two crazy dogs running to the café," complained Rick.

Aaron popped open the door to the café, looked back at Markie, and then barked. Aaron was very pleased to be showing Markie the ropes at the Doe Bay Café.

"I heard you coming up the path," said Mrs. Hamilton. She looked down and said, "Oh, who is your friend?"

Aaron barked and Mrs. Hamilton said to Markie, "Nice to meet you. Come outside fellas, I'll bring your dinner to the patio. Where's the boys – oh here comes Rick. He looks eager and hungry."

Mrs. Hamilton set down fresh water and crab cakes for Aaron. Markie sat down next to Aaron and watched him wolf them down.

"Hi Mrs. Hamilton," said Rick eagerly. "How do you like the robot dog Greg, Topher, and I built?"

"He is real cute. He almost seems real. One day Rick, you are going to be a famous computer programmer," she said with a smile. "Glad you boys found something else to do besides work. Tell, Greg and Topher your dinners will be ready shortly."

"Yes ma'am," replied Rick.

The boys were showing Mr. Hamilton their catch and he looked very pleased.

He said, "You mates are doing a great job. I am very happy with the job you have been doing. You are the best crabbers I ever had. Mrs. Hamilton will have your dinners ready soon. Come on in my office and I will pay you."

"Thanks sir," they responded.

Aaron was finished eating by the time they arrived at the picnic tables. He and Markie were walking around making sure that every blade of grass was marked.

Mr. Hamilton walked over to where the boys were sitting. Mrs. Hamilton had told him about the robot dog they made and he said, "Ain't your robot dog cute. Looks like you programmed him to mimic Aaron."

"Yes sir, we thought it would be funny," said Greg with a mouthful of the warm and delicious crab cakes.

The other boys nodded their heads.

"That is for sure. You mates are right clever," he said with a chuckle.

When the boys were finished eating they thanked Mrs. Hamilton and went on to see Captain MacArthur.

"Oh good, he is in his office," said Topher.

They walked into his office and Rick said, "Hey Captain MacArthur, how are you?"

"Not too bad," he answered. "What are you boys up to besides catching crabs for the Hamiltons?"

"Nothing much," replied Greg.

Markie and Aaron came into the office. Captain MacArthur looked at the robot dog and said, "Whoa, it looks like you have been up to more than just that!"

"Oh, yeah, we built the robot dog and he mimics things that Aaron does. Also, he is programmed for voice recognition," answered Topher.

"You boys did a great job!" Captain MacArthur responded.

"We were wondering, if we had the boat registration number of a boat, how do we find out who the owner of the boat is?" asked Rick.

Captain MacArthur looked at the boys with a question on his expression and said, "Well, I can run the numbers in my data base and it has a record of the name and address of the owner." He looked at the boys and continued, "Is someone giving you boys problems?"

"Oh, no sir," replied Greg. "We know most of the fishermen except two of them and we wondered who they are."

"Hmmm," said Captain MacArthur. "What's the registration numbers?"

Rick took out his notebook and read them to Captain MacArthur. The captain wrote them down and then turned to his computer and started looking them up.

Captain MacArthur said, "Wait a minute, I know these numbers. I looked them up the other day. Yes, the owner is John Graham of Seattle."

Captain MacArthur was getting ready to ask the boys what problems they were having with John Graham when his radio went off with an emergency distress call.

"Got to go," he yelled and started gathering his emergency kit in the outer office. He poked his head back into his office and said, "Some of the other fishermen have been complaining about him speeding in the No Wake Zones. I would like to talk to you about John Graham. Will you boys stop back in to see me tomorrow?"

The boys promised they would return tomorrow to talk to him as he was running out of the office. He waved his hand back to them to let them know that he had heard them.

The boys started out of Captain MacArthur's office when Topher looked over at his computer monitor and said, "Hey guys, look. There is more information about our mystery crabber in the data base. He owns both of the boats!"

The boys looked at the screen and read his street address and phone number.

Rick asked Markie to acess the information about John Graham from Captain MacArthur's computer. He nodded and began to transfer the data to his Internal Knowledge Unit using the computers wireless connection.

"Boy, I wish they had photos of the owners in the data base," said Greg.

"When we get back to the cabin let's try to look up

John Graham of Seattle in the different social media networks," said Topher.

"Good thinking," said Rick and Greg.

"Hopefully, we can find him and gather more intel," added Rick.

"Let's get some supplies for s'mores and have a bonfire tonight," said Greg.

Rick agreed, "Great, I do some of my best thinking with chocolate."

The boys laughed and nodded their heads. They chipped in their money and went to the market and bought graham crackers, two packages of chocolate bars, and a package of marshmallows.

Markie and Aaron followed them to the market and when the boys went inside the market, they waited outside. Markie was learning all about dog etiquette from Aaron. Whoever saw Markie just accepted him as the boys' robot dog. They thought it was funny when they saw Markie walking next to Aaron as if he were a real dog.

The boys were eager to get back to their cabin and start researching their mystery crabber. They wanted to look at the images Markie took. They were hoping to see exactly what it was the mystery crabber was getting out and putting into the crab pots. Also, they wanted to search the social media networks for any images or information on John Graham. As soon as they arrived at their cabin, they prepared the fire pit for their bonfire that evening and then went inside to review the intel they had gathered.

Chapter 9

Rick sat down at his computer and started searching the different social media networks for a John Graham.

"Wouldn't you know he would have a common name," he complained as he kept searching.

"Did you try limiting the search to the Seattle area?" asked Greg.

"Yep!" answered Rick.

Greg, Topher, and Markie were looking at the images from earlier in the day on Markie's chest plate screen.

"Zoom in over here," said Greg to Topher.

Topher enlarged the area Greg had pointed to and lightened the image.

"What is that?" asked Topher. "They appear to be

yellow rectangular blocks!"

"Markie can you scan the image with your Internal Knowledge Search Mode and tell us what they are?" asked Topher.

Markie scanned the image and said, "It is a solid substance and is one of the densest metals in existence on earth. It is listed in the Periodic Table as AU. The Latin name is Aurum, meaning Golden Dawn or Shining Dawn. I believe you call it simply – gold."

"Rick, did you hear that!" exclaimed Topher.

Rick turned away from his computer monitor to look at the image.

He looked at it and commented, "Oh my gosh!"

"I wonder how much each bar of gold is worth?" asked Greg.

Markie answered thoughtfully, "To calculate the value of each gold bar you need to know the weight of each bar. The value of gold is calculated by weight."

"How do we figure out how much each bar weighs?" asked Topher.

The boys were eagerly listening to Markie as he said, "First, it is important to know each cubic centimeter of pure gold weighs 19.3 grams. Using my scanner, I am able to determine the bars each measure six inches long by two inches wide by one inch high. Next, you would need to convert inches to centimeters."

Rick turned around and typed something into his computer and then proudly turned around and said, "There are approximately 2.54 centimeters in one inch."

"Yes, that is correct," said Markie. "Does anyone

know how you would figure the cubic centimeters in one cubic inch?"

"We studied exponents in school," said Greg with excitement. "Since we are calculating 2.54 cubed, we would multiply 2.54 times 2.54 times 2.54."

Topher started multiplying and came up with 16.387 cubic centimeters.

Markie asked the boys, "Is that the total weight of the bars of gold?"

"No," answered Rick. "You will have to multiply 16.387 times 12, because there are twelve cubic inches in each bar."

Greg did the multiplication and came up with an answer of 196.64 for the total cubic centimeters for each bar.

Markie nodded his head and the boys were happy to be able to do the calculations and understand the concept.

Markie continued, "Now that you know the size of the bars, you have to multiply the total cubic centimeters for each bar times what?"

"The weight of one cubic centimeter, which is......... 19.3!" shouted Rick with excitement.

Quickly, the boys started multiplying 19.3 times 196.64 and the result was 3,795 grams.

"But, how do we know how much it is worth?" asked Topher eagerly.

"I'll search online and see what the current rate of gold is per gram," announced Rick.

Rick looked it up on the internet as the boys stood behind him. He found the amount and Greg did the calculations.

Greg, sounding like an expert said, "Estimating the current price of 3,795 grams of pure gold, I would say each bar is worth about ... are you guys ready for this ... $175,000."

The boys were stunned and Markie was watching their reactions. Aaron jumped up and down as he sensed their excitement.

Topher looked at the image again and said, "There are at least 4 or more bars in this crab pot! If there were that many bars in each crab pot, then our mystery crabber has taken in over two million dollars in gold!"

Rick's computer was busy searching several social media sites and finally pinged on a John Graham in Seattle. He was found on a business social network. There was a small photo of John Graham, but it was hard to tell if that was their John Graham.

Rick clicked on John Graham's bio and when his larger photo appeared on the screen they said, "Oh my gosh, it's him!"

"He works at the Northern Bank of Seattle as the New Accounts and Safety Deposit Box Manager," read Rick out loud.

"What would a manager at a bank be doing with gold bars?" asked Topher.

"I don't think banks just keep gold bars around," stated Greg.

They were sitting on the edge of their seats in a tense state. Suddenly, their marine radio started to make a static sound. They jumped out of their seats.

A familiar voice came over their marine radio, "Rick,

this is Captain MacArthur. Are you boys home? Over."

Rick replied promptly, "Yes, Captain. Over"

"You forgot your bait on the docks earlier and I will come to your cabin and drop it off to you. Over."

Rick looked at Topher and Greg and said, "Bait? What is he talking about?"

"Maybe it is code for something else," suggested Greg.

To the Captain, Rick responded, "Thank you, sir. Over."

"No problem, I am already on my way there and I'll see you in a few minutes. Over," replied Captain MacArthur.

"Wow, talk about perfect timing," said Greg. "I think we have enough information to share with Captain MacArthur when he arrives. What do you both think?"

Rick and Topher nodded their heads in agreement.

"Let's go down to the docks and help the Captain with his lines. Then, we will invite him to come up to the cabin and share our findings with him," said Topher.

The boys headed down to the docks, but were surprised when Captain MacArthur came around the cove with his personal boat and not the Coast Guard boat. Furthermore, he had his civilian clothes on.

"Hi boys," said Captain MacArthur as he handed the line to Greg.

"Hey Captain, we almost didn't recognize you without your Coast Guard boat," said Topher softly. He was sensing the Captain was not there to drop off bait for the crabs.

In an unusually loud voice, Captain MacArthur

answered, "Yeah, I heard you boys forgot to take your crab bait, so I brought it over to you. Let's go into the house and put it in the refrigerator before the crabs start crawling on land to get it."

Aaron was scratching at the front door and whining. Rick had latched the door from the outside, so that Aaron couldn't get out. He was a little spooked by the happenings and didn't want Aaron outside running around. When Aaron whined he made a chirping sound. As they approached the cabin, they could hear Aaron making his chirping sound.

The Captain opened the door and said, "Hey boy, I am happy to see you too," and then gave Aaron a rub behind the ears. To the boys he said, "Oh, here is your bait!"

Rick took the bag and looked inside and said, "Oh neat, chocolate chip cookies! Somehow, I don't think the bait is for the crabs. I think the bait is for us."

Captain MacArthur nodded his head and said, "OK boys, what's up? I have known you all long enough to know that something is going on."

"Sir, we didn't want to come to you until we had enough information," said Greg.

"Fair enough," he said. "Why don't you share with me the information that you have gathered?"

"Your timing couldn't have been any better. We have just finished putting a major piece of the puzzle together and we were getting ready to call you," replied Rick.

"We need to take you up to the dormitory, our command center, and show you the intel that we have gathered so far," said Topher.

Captain MacArthur smiled at them having a command center and intel. The boys led Captain MacArthur to the dormitory and when he walked in the room he said, "Oh wow, this is a sophisticated intel operation."

The boys had maps, charts, and images on their cork board. Captain MacArthur walked over to the cork board and told them he was impressed at their thoroughness. While the Captain was busy looking at their intel, Aaron went and sat down next to him. Slowly and quietly, Markie came out from his hiding place behind one of the beds and sat down next to Aaron.

Captain looked down and said, "Hey little fella, how are you? What are you calling him?"

"Markie," answered Rick.

The Captain was watching Markie and then looked at the boys with a smirk on his face, "Your Markie doesn't look like a typical toy robot, but somehow I think he is a story for another time."

"Can we keep that just between us?" requested Rick.

Captain MacArthur said, "Sure."

Captain turned his attention back to the cork board. The boys went through their complete run down of facts as they knew them. Captain had taken out his notepad and was taking notes as they boys were sharing their facts. Captain MacArthur examined each piece of evidence very carefully and wrote down the information.

Rick concluded by saying, "We have a banker who

appears to be fencing gold to someone, but where did he get the gold and who is his fence?"

"You did a great job of gathering your intel. How did you communicate with each other over the marine radio without him hearing you?" inquired the Captain.

"He might have heard us, but he probably didn't know what we were saying," answered Topher.

"Why is that?" asked the Captain.

"Well, we were communicating using Morse code signals. You know like the distress call S.O.S.," said Greg.

The Captain continued his inquiry, "How did you boys learn Morse code?"

Without thinking Topher said, "Markie taught us Morse code."

The Captain looked at Markie, scrunched his eyebrows down, and said, "Hmmmm, you are talking about the toy robot, Markie?"

"Yes, Markie taught us Morse code. That part is true, but the toy robot part may be a stretch," answered Rick truthfully. "But, you agreed we could talk about that at a later time." Rick smiled at the Captain.

The Captain looked at Markie and Markie smiled at him. The Captain rolled his eyes and wiped his forehead.

"The first thing I need to do is to call my contact with the FBI and local police authorities," said Captain MacArthur. "I want you to know how impressed I am with the quality of research that you boys have done on this case."

The Captain put the FBI and local authorities on a

three-way conversation to discuss the case. The boys were nearby and could hear bits and pieces of the conversation. He must have been asked how he was able to gather all the information about the banker and his accomplice and he replied, "Let's just say the S.O.S. Boys followed a hunch and then gathered the intel for me." He then continued a few minutes later by saying, "Yes, the intel is very thorough and credible. Thank you, I will tell them."

After what seemed like an eternity the Captain was off the phone.

"Boys, it is getting late and I am going to spend the night. I am going to call my wife and let her know that I will spend the night here," said the Captain.

"Captain, would you tell her not to call our parents. We don't want to worry them unnecessarily," requested Topher.

"I will tell her the information is confidential and that you boys are safe," he assured them.

After calling his wife he said, "The FBI is going to put an agent in the bank tomorrow to watch the suspect. Based on your intel, he won't be coming out here for at least two days."

The boys nodded their heads and agreed with the captains reasoning. They also thought he probably won't return for a couple days.

"Tomorrow, I am going to set up a meeting with the FBI and the local authorities to go over your intel. Also, I will need to get an agreement for a sting operation, so we can identify any new suspects," said Captain MacArthur.

Rick suggested, "If you need any help, we would be happy to help you."

Greg and Topher shook their heads in agreement.

"I am glad you boys feel that way. Tomorrow at the meeting with the FBI and local authorities, I want you to lead the discussion on your intel information. We may also need your help out on the water. You would each be imbedded with an agent," answered the Captain.

The boys were excited to be part of the sting operation.

"It's getting late and we should get some sleep. Tomorrow will be a busy day," announced the Captain.

The boys agreed and headed up to bed. It was a little hard for them to get to sleep and they had to explain to Markie what a sting operation is. Markie asked if he could go too and they agreed he was critical to the operation.

Aaron tilted his head as if to ask if he were invited too and Rick said, "Yes, you are going too!"

Aaron barked and jumped up on the bed.

After the boys got into bed, they kept talking about the sting operation and how cool it was they were going to explain their intel with the FBI!

"It looks like we are now the S.O.S. Boys," said Greg.

"Yep!" chimed in Rick, Topher, Markie, and a bark from Aaron in agreement.

Chapter 10

Aaron's head popped up from where he was laying on the bed with Rick. He heard Captain MacArthur stirring around on the first floor. He jumped off the bed and made his way downstairs. Markie was not far behind him.

Captain MacArthur looked at the dogs and said, "I suppose you want to go outside."

He walked over, opened the door, and to his surprise Markie followed Aaron outside. He stepped out on the porch to watch the dogs and was amused as Markie followed Aaron around mimicking his actions. Within a short time, Aaron and Markie returned to the cabin. The Captain let them inside and proceeded to set Aaron's food out.

He looked at Markie and said jokingly, "Sorry boy, I don't know what toy robots eat."

Markie looked at him and said, "Me either, but I don't require human or dog food."

The Captain almost spilled the coffee he was drinking and said, "What?"

Markie realized what he had said and then started to walk around like a toy robot dog. Next, he moved his head stiffly like one.

The Captain laughed and said, "OK. OK. I get it. You are a toy robot dog. No questions."

Markie looked at him, smiled, and nodded his head.

The Captain continued, "When I am not here, keep an eye on the boys and Aaron for me. OK?"

Markie nodded his head in agreement and said, "Yes, sir captain."

The Captain shook his head, took a deep breath, and thought to himself out loud, one day, I will want to know everything the boys have been up to.

The boys heard the Captain on the phone. They quickly got dressed and headed downstairs. They wanted to make sure they didn't miss anything exciting going on.

Captain heard them running down the stairs and said to them as they entered the kitchen, "Glad you boys are up early. We are going to have a busy day today. The FBI and the local authorities are arriving in an hour. I thought it would be easier for them to come here and look at your intel."

The boys were excited the Captain was taking them seriously and was involving them in the sting operation.

"Cool," they responded.

As soon as they had finished breakfast and getting ready for the FBI and local authorities, they heard the sound of the engines from the boats arriving. The boys were excited and ran down to the docks with Aaron and Markie following them. They wanted to help the agents and officers with their lines. They were not surprised they were dressed like fishermen and were in fishing boats.

Captain MacArthur was also there to greet them and lead them up to the cabin. There were four FBI agents, two Coast Guard personnel, and two police officers.

Captain MacArthur said, "Gentleman, I will have the boys show you to their command center. They have gathered extensive information on the suspects."

The agents and police followed the boys upstairs.

Agent Nathan Oliver looked at the cork board and said, "Wow, you boys have done a great job of gathering detailed intel on the suspects."

The boys smiled and thanked him. They were feeling proud of their hard work and in-depth research.

Agent Oliver asked them to explain the information as the officers, agents, and Coast Guard personnel began to take notes.

Topher, Rick, and Greg each took turns sharing their intel. Captain MacArthur was smiling and proud of the way the boys were conducting their information sharing meeting.

Agent Thompson said, "How old are you boys?"

"We're 15 years old, sir," answered Greg.

"I know I can speak for everyone here when I say what

an exceptional job you boys have done in recognizing that something was not right with these crabbers. Also, you boys did a thorough job of gathering your intel and figuring out what these criminals were up to," said Agent Oliver.

The boys were beaming from ear to ear.

Agent Oliver then turned to Captain MacArthur and said, "I think we will need to imbed each of the boys with one of our agents and officers. The mystery crabbers, as the boys have named them, are already used to seeing them and their boat. We don't want to spook them and scare them off."

Captain responded, "I agree and I think they will do a great job."

"Oh, there is no question of that," said Agent Oliver.

Using the map, images, and charts, the agents and officers began to make a plan to catch the mystery crabber and his accomplice.

Rick pointed to the map and made a suggestion as to where the boats should be placed and who should be in the different boats. Rick concluded by saying that Aaron and two agents should be in the boys' boat. He told them the mystery crabbers have always seen the three boys and Aaron in their boat and any change might make them suspicious.

Agent Oliver said, "Yes, that is a good plan."

Then Markie barked a mechanical bark as if to say, don't forget about me.

Topher added, "Markie should be in the boat with me and he can help us send Morse code signals."

Markie looked eagerly at Captain MacArthur and

the Captain responded, "Perhaps he could be in my boat. The robot dog is fast at sending Morse code. He would be a valuable asset to me."

"Sounds good to me," said Agent Oliver.

Markie looked up at Captain MacArthur and the boys and smiled.

Topher and Greg were each going to be with an officer and an agent in the other boats.

The FBI agents and officers knew they needed to send messages to each other and were going to rely on the boys' knowledge and skill of sending Morse code signals to communicate instead of the police radios.

While the agents and officers completed their logistics for the sting operation, the boys decided to go over their abbreviated Morse code signals and practiced sending them to each other.

For the next couple of days before the sting operation, the boys continued with their routine of crabbing and visiting the Hamiltons. They didn't want to raise any suspicion by changing their schedule.

The agent imbedded at Northern Bank of Seattle had been watching John Graham for two days. The report from the agent was that John Graham was in and out of the safety deposit box area of the bank a lot. Every time the agent walked by the safety deposit box area, John Graham would leave quickly. The agent made a note that he was visiting the same box. After doing some research at the bank, the agent was able to learn it was not John Graham's safety deposit box, but a box belonging to an elderly woman named Mrs. Edith Remfern. In addition, there appeared to be something heavy in his sport coat pocket when he left the safety deposit box area.

After observing the unusual behavior of John Graham at the bank, the agent suggested the sting operation should be set for Wednesday.

On Wednesday morning, the boys were filled with adrenaline as they woke up at 4 AM. The plan was for the boys to be in the different boats by 4:30 AM. The boys had made a prediction as to where the mystery crabbers would appear. They were hoping they were right. The sting operation depended on it.

Once the boys, agents, officers, and dogs were in position, they began to send each other a Morse code signal announcing they were in position.

Markie and Captain MacArthur were in a boat located on the southwest coast of Cypress Island. Rick, Aaron, and Agents Oliver and Snyder were in a boat in Lost Cove. Greg and Officer Morris's boat was located on the northwest coast of Blakely Island. Topher and Officer Lopez's boat was situated on the northeast coast of Sinclair Island. Markie and Captain MacArthur were the last to get into position. Markie sent the boys the message that he and the Captain were in position.

Markie turned to Captain MacArthur and said, "I sent them the message we are in position. Do you want me to tell them anything else?"

"Yes, tell them I am proud of them," said the Captain.

Markie smiled and sent them the message. They sent a message back: *dah   dah dit dit dah,   dit dit dah,* TX U, which was thank you.

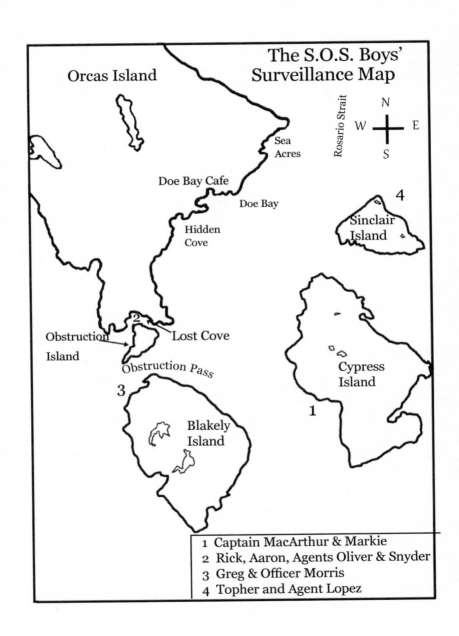

The S.O.S. Boys' Surveillance Map

Orcas Island

Rosario Strait

N
W + E
S

Sea Acres

Doe Bay Cafe

Doe Bay

4
Sinclair Island

Hidden Cove

2
Obstruction Island → Lost Cove

Obstruction Pass

3
Blakely Island

Cypress Island

1

1 Captain MacArthur & Markie
2 Rick, Aaron, Agents Oliver & Snyder
3 Greg & Officer Morris
4 Topher and Agent Lopez

Each minute seemed to pass like an hour. The water was relatively calm, as they sat patiently bobbing up and down in the water. The longer the time passed the more anxious they became.

Rick said with a slight chuckle to the agents, "I can hear my heart pounding louder than the waves splashing up against the boat."

Agent Oliver smiled and said, "Yeah, I know what you mean. I have been on many stake outs and as you get closer to the time the action is going to take place the more adrenaline pumps through your body. You boys are doing a great job."

A small boat bearing the registration numbers RH0521TE zoomed past them. Remembering the boys intel, Captain MacArthur knew that it was the boat John Graham used. He had Markie send a Morse code signal announcing John Graham was on the move on the west coast of Cypress Island.

Then, within a short time, Greg and Officer Morris saw the boat heading towards Lost Cove. Greg sent the following message: *dah dit dah dit,   dit dah dah dah dah dah dit,* C JG.

Rick and Topher understood Greg could see John Graham arriving and according to the reports from both Captain MacArthur and Greg, he was headed for Lost Cove.

As John Graham entered Lost Cove, he looked around at Rick, Aaron, Agents Oliver and Snyder. He thought it was the same three boys and dog he had seen many times before dropping crab pots in the water. They pretended to be busy with their crab pots and not watching him. John Graham wanted to put the gold bars into the crab pots quickly, lower them into the water, and get out of there.

He was fumbling around with the gold bars and the crab pots. There was a loud clunk sound as he dropped one of the bars on the floor of the boat. He nervously looked around again, but no one seemed to be watching him.

As John Graham was ready to drop the crab pots into the water, Agent Oliver was able to look over quickly and see the gold bars in the pot. With a hidden camera he had set-up earlier, he took a photo of it as proof.

Once the crab pots were lowered and the buoys were bobbing in the water, he looked around again, and took off.

Rick sent the following message to Topher, Greg Captain MacArthur, the agents, and officers: *dit dah dah dah   dah dah dit,   dah dit dit   dit dah dit   dit dah dah dit,   dit dah dit dit   dit   dit dit dit dah,* JG DRP LEV, which meant John Graham had dropped his crab pots and was leaving.

Greg watched as John Graham headed out of the cove and traveled southwest. He quickly sent the following message: *dit dah dah dah   dah dah dit,   dit dit dit   dit dah dah,* JG SW.

Greg and Officer Morris watched as John Graham maintained his southwest direction along the west coast of Cypress Island.

Since Captain MacArthur was positioned farther down the west coast of Cypress Island, he and Markie were able to keep an eye on where John Graham was headed.

Captain MacArthur set a course such that John Graham would pass them. Then Captain MacArthur could continue to follow him without being detected.

There were agents positioned farther out on either side of the island and prepared to follow him. They didn't want to nab him just yet, but follow him and see where he went. They wanted to see if there were any other accomplices involved in the crime. Also, they didn't know if he had to notify mystery crabber 2 that he had made the drop. The agents wanted to be able to catch both of them and not to disrupt their plans.

Everyone was on alert for mystery crabber 2. Captain MacArthur and Markie were slowly following John Graham when without warning; he slowed down and appeared to be pulling into a small cove along Cypress Island.

"Markie send everyone the message that John Graham has pulled into a small cove on the west coast of Cypress Island," ordered Captain MacArthur. "Let them know that we are going to stay around and see what he does."

Captain MacArthur told Markie he thought John Graham was going to wait in the cove until the money is dropped and then go back and get it.

It was about an hour later, when Topher sent the following message: *dah dah,   dit dah   dit dah dit dit dit dit dah,   dit dit dit   dit,* M ARV SE, so mystery crabber 2 was arriving from the southeast. So far, all was going according to plan.

Rick, Aaron, and Agents Oliver and Snyder were inside the cove. Once again, they pretended to be crabbing when mystery crabber 2 pulled into the cove.

Agent Oliver said, "Rick start the engine up and let's slowly leave the cove, but set a heading so I can have a clear view of the starboard side of his boat. I am going to try and get a photo of what he is doing."

Rick was nervous. He had to keep telling himself starboard, starboard. He did as agent Oliver had ordered and slowly steered the boat out of the cove.

Mystery crabber 2 pulled up the crab pots and quickly took the gold bars out. Next, he put the black bag into the pot. He lowered the crab pots down, started up his engine, and took off. Since there was no one else in the cove he moved confidently and without concern.

Rick quickly sent the Morse code signal that mystery crabber 2 was leaving and traveling southeast. Topher and his agent began traveling southeast. Mystery crabber 2 held his course and headed for the east coast of Sinclair Island.

Topher sent a Morse code signal about the direction mystery crabber 2 was heading. An agent located on the east coast of Sinclair Island continued the pursuit. He hung back far enough to keep an eye on his direction and not alert him to the fact that he was being followed.

As soon as mystery crabber 2 rounded Sinclair Island, he must have notified John Graham the drop was made because Captain MacArthur had Markie send the following Morse code signal: *dit dah dah dah, dah dit dah dit   dah dah dah   dah dah,   dah dit dit dit   dit dah   dah dit dah,* J COM BAK.

The agents following mystery crabber 2, dropped their extra engine in the water and headed out to catch up with him. The boat flew on the water and they were able to catch up to mystery crabber 2 within a short time.

Using a bull horn an agent yelled, "STOP, FBI. Put your hands up in the air and don't move."

They pulled alongside mystery crabber 2's boat. They boarded the boat and found five gold bars on the floor of the boat.

Rick was idling his engine at the entrance to the cove. Aaron started to bark and Rick knew that meant John Graham's boat was approaching the cove. Agent Oliver told Rick to slowly steer his boat out of the cove and was directed to head towards the southwest. They wanted it to appear that he was just leaving.

Meanwhile, the trap was being set for John Graham inside the cove. As John Graham entered the cove and approached his crab pots, three boats of agents and officers waited at the outlet to the cove. Another agent was positioned at the top of the cliff that overlooked the cove. He had a clear view of John Graham and the contents of his boat and crab pots. He took photos of what John Graham was doing. After the pots and black plastic bag filled with money were loaded into his boat, the agent signaled the agents in the other boats to rush into the cove to make the arrest.

In a short time, the following message was relayed over the marine radio: "Thanks to the S.O.S. Boys we have both suspects in custody."

The fishermen in the area heard the message and

began to speculate what was going on. It would be a few days before everyone heard how a group of boys called: The S.O.S. Boys, assisted the FBI, Coast Guards, and local police officers to solve a major gold heist and capture the criminals.

Mystery crabber 2, aka Freddie Smythe, was arrested under suspicion of taking stolen goods. John Graham was arrested for stealing gold bars from Mrs. Edith Remfern's safety deposit box and receiving money for the stolen gold.

Captain MacArthur had put a call into the boys' parents and asked them to meet him at their cabin that afternoon. When the parents arrived, they could tell something important had happened.

Once they were in Rick's parent's cabin, Captain MacArthur told them what the boys had done to solve a huge gold heist and capture the criminals. The parents were astounded at what the boys had done. They had a million questions to ask the boys. The boys spent the afternoon filling in all the details of the crime with their parents.

Anna Taylor asked Captain MacArthur, "Are the boys in any danger from cracking the case?"

Captain MacArthur responded, "No, because we are going to refer to the boys as the S.O.S. Boys. If we keep their identity a secret there won't be any problems. The boys did a great job of gathering the intel. The FBI agents were very impressed."

Susan asked, "Why the S.O.S. Boys?"

Topher answered, "Because we communicated with each other using Morse code signals – you know like

S.O.S." He tapped out: *dit dit dit   dah dah dah   dit dit dit.* "We thought if we used Morse code the criminals wouldn't know what we were saying to each other as we reported to each other what they were doing."

Greg Sr. said, "That is very clever of you boys. How did you learn Morse code?"

Rick replied, "From Markie our robot dog."

Everyone looked over at Markie and he sat very still. Captain MacArthur looked over at him and winked.

Throughout the evening, the families talked about the gold heist and how clever the boys were in solving the mystery.

A few weeks later...

The boys continued working for the Hamiltons catching crabs and were always on the lookout for a mystery to solve.

Markie would watch everyone and say, "Is he supposed to be doing that? Is that a criminal?"

Markie was also studying all the rules of the sea and let the boys know what infractions he would see other fishermen doing.

Rick said, "I think we have created a monster in Markie."

Greg and Topher laughed and said to Markie, "You are doing a great job. Keep it up. We never know when a mystery will fall into our laps."

Markie nodded and Aaron barked. They were both on high alert status.

They were surprised when Captain MacArthur hailed them over the marine radio and told them he wanted to see them and their parents. They set a time and when he arrived, Aaron greeted him at the dock before the boys could get there. Of course, Markie was standing next to him. The boys had run down to the docks to help Captain MacArthur with his lines.

"Hey boys," he said.

"Hey Captain, what's up?" they asked.

"Something you and your parents will be happy to hear," he responded.

Captain MacArthur went up to the cabin with an envelope and package under his arm.

"Come on in," said Rick's dad.

The parents were in the family room when he walked in.

Captain MacArthur said, "The bank has learned about how your boys were able to help capture John Graham and his accomplice and they have issued a reward of $60,000 for the boys."

"Wow!" said the boys.

Greg said, "We want to give it to our parents."

The parents looked at each other, shook their heads, and told the boys it would go towards their college fund.

Then Captain MacArthur said, "Oh, I have a package from Mrs. Edith Remfern for the S.O.S. Boys. Topher took the package and the boys opened it up together. Inside the package was the following note:

Dear S.O.S. Boys,

Thank you for catching the men who were trying to steal my gold bars. I was on a month long trip to see my sister in Austria. By the time I would have returned, he would have stolen all of my gold bars.

Please accept this as a token of my appreciation.

Mrs. Edith Remfern

They opened up the box and inside were one of the six inches long by two inches wide by one inch high solid gold bar that had been divided into three equal pieces.

"OMG!" was the gasp from everyone in the room.

The parents said in unison, "College Fund!"

The boys smiled and were excited and began jumping up and down. Aaron was barking and Markie sat and watched everyone. He smiled at Captain MacArthur.

The Captain walked over, patted Markie on the head, and said, "Remember, keep an eye on them for me."

Markie said quietly, "Yes sir!"

When the weekend was over and the parents had left to return to the mainland, the boys went and dropped their crab pots in the water, as usual, with Aaron and Markie in tow. Afterwards, they headed into Doe Bay to get some cookies from the Sweet Treat Bakery. Markie had become a regular in Doe Bay and no one even questioned him. They were always amused at how he followed Aaron around. Of course, Markie was always careful not to say anything when he was around other people.

"I can smell the double chocolate chip cookies all the way out here," said Greg as they came close to the bakery. The boys and the dogs entered the bakery. Mrs. Sweet had just finished making her double chocolate chip cookies.

When they selected their cookies, Rick said, "Hey guys, I got this. I have some extra change."

He reached in his wallet and pulled out his coins. When he was counting out his change, he saw a strange looking coin.

He paid Mrs. Sweet and as he was walking outside he said to Topher and Greg, "Guys, check out this strange looking coin. Doesn't it look like it is gold?"

After examining it Greg said, "Yeah it does. Wow it has odd writing on it and looks very old."

"Let me see it," said Topher and added, "Very strange indeed."

"I wonder where I got it from," pondered Rick as he held it up for another look.

Greg started to laugh and said, "I think we have our next mystery to solve."

And this begins the next adventure of the S.O.S. Boys...